HER BEST FRIEND FAKE FIANCÉ: BENTON BILLIONAIRE SERIES

BENTON BROTHER ROMANCE

KIMBERLY KREY

Candle
House
Publishing

CHAPTER 1

en Years Ago

Sawyer glanced casually around the roomful of guests and noticed, without effort, that Betzy was missing. Must have snuck off to the restroom.

Music thumped loud over the chatter as he weaved toward the drink station—brown-tinted bottles of nonalcoholic fake beer, a selection of energy drinks, and an array of iced cold coffees. The sight alone, surrounded by solo cups and ice buckets, screamed parent-chaperoned graduation party. And that it was—combined with his own farewell gathering—courtesy of Sawyer's insistent mother.

And though he was surrounded by a few dozen of his finest friends, Sawyer couldn't shake the odd emptiness that hovered beyond the crowd. He always figured he'd be excited about trading his laid-back life on the west coast for fast-paced living in New York City, but he hadn't known how hard it would be to say goodbye to all that he'd known.

The distinct jostle of the bathroom door gained Sawyer's attention in a blink. A tall blonde stepped out of the doorway as it swung open. *Dang, not Betzy. It was Daisy.*

"Got a little something to put in those drinks?" came a voice from behind.

Sawyer looked over his shoulder to see Duke standing there. "Uh, if you ask around, I'm sure you'll find something." He motioned to a couple of his rowdier friends.

Duke followed his gaze to where the crowd huddled beside one of the speakers. "Thanks."

"Hey, wait," Sawyer blurted. Not that the kid kept track of his sister, but it was worth a try. "Do you know where Betzy ran off to?"

Duke nodded. "She's out back. Think she's pretty upset that you're leaving."

The way that he'd said it, so nonchalant and matter-of-fact, contrasted the response happening in Sawyer's chest. Pulse pounding. Heart racing.

"Why would she be upset?"

Duke, who'd already started walking toward the group, shot him a questioning look. "Because you guys have been, like, best friends most of her life. Sheesh."

But Sawyer couldn't let it go so easily. "Yeah, but she's been blowing me off all week. I wasn't even sure she'd bother coming to this."

Duke shook his head and shrugged. "Women."

"Hi, Sawyer," Daisy said, joining the small huddle. "Hi,

Duke." The blonde rested one hand on Sawyer's shoulder, the other on Duke's. "Which one of you handsome guys would like to walk this girl onto the dance floor?"

Sawyer gave Duke a look, one he hoped said *she's all yours.*

Duke furrowed his brow and eyed the modest-sized room. "Uh, it's not much of a dance floor, but I will." Relief washed over Sawyer as Duke shot Daisy a wink and wrapped a hand around her waist. "C'mon."

"Fine," she said with a sigh. But before she was dragged off to the dance area, Daisy rushed in and pressed a kiss to Sawyer's cheek. "*You* owe me the next one."

Sawyer didn't bother replying as he stepped away, eyes already set on the door leading to the patio out back. No guy liked being toyed with by their ex-girlfriend. Period. Especially in front of his buddies. Besides, Sawyer sensed there was some sort of rivalry between Betzy and Daisy; he wanted to be clear about where his loyalty lay.

If he were being honest, something else was bothering him too. Duke's comment about the inadequate dance area fed that monster of insecurity. A monster that appeared the moment Sawyer realized he was different from the kids at his prestigious private school.

While nearly every student lived posh lives—complete with massive estates, endless funds, and housemaids who picked up after them—Sawyer was born to a different sort of life. In fact, his mother *was* the housemaid. She'd worked for the Benton family from the time Sawyer was just two years old.

Generous as the billionaire family was, Claudia and Jonathon Benton paid for Sawyer to attend the finest private education money could buy—the very school their own children attended.

Of course, that's not where he and Betzy became friends. That happened before they ever started school, when he lived in the staff's quarters on the Benton Estate.

Sawyer's hand felt numb as he gripped the knob and gave it a twist. What would he say to her?

Are you really upset that I'm leaving, like Duke said?

I'm going to miss you like crazy.

I want you to know that...that I'm doing this for you.

"Sawyer?"

The sound of his name made him freeze in place halfway between the kitchen and the outdoor deck. "Hey, Mom." His shoulders fell flat, an action his mom followed with a concerned look.

"What's wrong?" she asked. "Aren't you having a good time?"

"No, I am. Of course." He nodded and blew out a breath. *Please don't ask me to refill the ice buckets right now.*

She didn't. Instead, she tipped her head to look past him. Not that she'd see anything, as dark as it was. "Who's out there?"

Great. "Um, maybe Betzy. Duke said she might be out here." He threw a thumb over his shoulder.

Mom grinned. "Oh. Good."

An uneasy sigh passed through his lips. "Okay."

"Hey," Mom said. "Be gentle with her, okay? She, um...this is probably pretty hard for her. Heck, you guys have been in love since you were old enough to talk."

"*Mom*," Sawyer hissed under his breath. Heat filled his neck and cheeks. "That was forever ago."

His mom swept a blonde lock of her hair behind one ear and leaned in. "Well, if you're leaving her behind to go make a name for yourself," she said in a whisper, "you better leave her with something to remember you with."

Sawyer shook his head. "Like what—jewelry? You know I can't compete—"

But she swatted him on the arm before he could finish. "Like a *kiss*, dummy. A *good* one. Now get out of here."

A groan made its way to his throat as he hurried out the door at last. If Betzy was standing within earshot, he'd rather jump off the balcony's edge and hitchhike to the airport than have to face the embarrassment.

The soft creaking of the swing set out back said she might not have heard after all. Thank heavens.

Sawyer tucked his hands into his pockets as he took the wood-slatted steps, peering into the darkness below. There was likely enough light at his back that she could see his silhouette, but it wasn't enough to reach the swing set. He only hoped it was actually her.

"Betz?" he hollered, testing.

"Sawyer?" She sounded surprised. "What are you doing out here?"

He shrugged, eyes adjusting as he approached the neglected swing set. "Maybe I'm looking for you."

"Maybe?"

Sawyer stepped up to the swing beside hers, looped a hand around the cool, metal chain, and sank onto the seat. It stayed quiet as he watched her carve lines into the dirt with the toe of her shoe.

"It feels weird that you're leaving," she said, voice soft and small.

He nodded.

"I mean, you used to talk about it. I just didn't think it'd actually happen."

Sawyer weighed her words, not sure what she meant by them. He'd never wavered in his pursuit for success. Had she seen him as a big talker or a dreamer? Incapable of following through?

"I just don't see why it has to be so far away. There's plenty of real estate in California. Why does it have to be New York?"

A spark of warmth flared in his chest. She didn't want him to leave. He liked that. With the new dose of encouragement pushing him on, he gripped hold of the chains, reared back a few steps, and began to pump. "Swing with me."

"Will you answer my question if I do?"

"Maybe."

Betzy started to back the swing up, but she stopped at his reply. "I'm not going to swing with you if you don't."

He chuckled. "This feels like the good old days, doesn't it?"

"Yeah." She plunked onto her swing and began to pump. "It does. I miss it."

More heat brewed low in his belly. "I miss it too. As for the New York thing, it's what I've always planned on. My uncle's one of the biggest real estate tycoons in the business, and he's going to teach me everything he knows. Why not learn from the best?"

He swooshed past her a few times, back and forth, before finally matching her pace.

"Yeah, but you don't *have* to be rich."

"Says the girl from the billionaire family. The one who just inherited her first million..."

"I *invested* my first million and...and you know that's not important to me, right?"

Sawyer didn't reply. What could he say, that he didn't believe her? "I can still make you marry me either way," he said, thinking back on the silly document they'd constructed years back.

"Are you talking about the marriage contract?" she said with a laugh. "Oh, I can't believe we did that. I reeled you right in, didn't I?"

Sawyer was about to lean back and pump the swing higher, but her words stopped him short. He let his feet hit the dirt once, then twice before he stopped. "What do you mean? The whole marriage contract was *my* idea."

That cute little laugh of hers toppled from her lips. "*That's* how I reeled you in. I got you to do it, *and* think it was your idea too."

He'd have to consider that some more. The way he saw it, it was all his idea, all the way down to the determined age the marriage should take place—twenty-eight years old. Two significant events took place because of that contract, events that catapulted Sawyer toward one life-changing choice.

The first came when Sawyer boasted the contract to his wealthy Uncle Ryan.

Sawyer could hear his response even still. *Oh, no, little buddy. You can't marry into money unless you have money of your own. You better come work for me if you want to get a chick like that.*

While he'd gotten crap from his uncle about the impossibilities of marrying Betzy, she was getting an earful from her mother. One Sawyer had, by accident, overheard.

I'm not mad about the contract, sweetie. I think it's cute. We love Sawyer too. But you're a Benton, don't forget that. When you come from money, you don't marry the housemaid's son. You just don't.

Sure, the woman was kind to him. Very. And Sawyer had told himself that Claudia had likely changed her position over the years, but he couldn't be sure.

Either way, those two instances sparked a determination like none he'd ever known. He *would* go work for Uncle Ryan. And then, he'd come back and marry Betzy when he was ready.

"I'm going to jump," Betzy announced, pulling him from his musings. "Should I do it?"

"I wouldn't," Sawyer said as he looked into the darkness. Sure, his eyes had adjusted enough to see her right beside him, but the wider part of the yard looked like one black hole.

Betzy started counting. "One..."

"What if you run into the lawn mower or something?" he asked.

"Two..." she continued.

Sawyer came to a stand and wiped his hands on his jeans. If Betzy said she was going to jump, that meant she would jump, alright.

"Three!" And there she went, flying right out of her swing and into the darkness. "Woo-hoo," she hollered from a spot across the yard.

Sawyer squinted, trying to catch sight of her white, summer dress while an odd knot of longing pulled at him from the inside. He'd miss this. Miss hanging out with the girl who'd captured him in every possible way.

It had put him in a tough spot. He couldn't date her until he had money. But how was he supposed to keep her in his life without getting permanently placed in the friend zone?

Inevitably, he'd dated other girls. She'd dated other guys, and they'd spent less time together over the years, which seemed to support Uncle Ryan's notion—he needed to make money, make a name for himself, and *then* maybe he'd have a shot.

Well, that's just what he planned to do.

But maybe...just maybe what his mom said was true. Heck, the friend zone was a very real thing, and if he was taking off the next few years, Sawyer may as well leave Betzy with something that went far beyond friendship.

Betzy snuck quietly across the grass toward the shed in Sawyer's yard, hoping he hadn't detected her movement as he called for her.

"Betz, you there?" He sounded worried now. She chuckled under her breath as she made her way through the high, grassy weeds between the fence and the shed.

"What, we're playing hide and seek now?" he asked, sounding amused.

It took everything in her not to laugh out loud. Betzy knew she was being silly, but spending this time with Sawyer brought out the kid in her. Made her want to do things like jump out of her swing, hide behind the shed, and jump out at him once she got to the other side, something she totally planned on doing next.

She moved to take another step when her foot got snagged in a tangled patch of weeds. If she wasn't careful she'd fall on her face, but as she lifted her foot higher to free it from the growth, her hip bumped the shed and tipped her off balance.

Frantically, she spun to face the fence, hoping to catch the chain link with her fingers, when suddenly a strong set of arms caught her from behind. "Gotcha!"

It was Sawyer, and yes, he did. That heavenly scent of his aftershave confirmed it, if the strength of his solid arms didn't say enough. And while it startled her—enough to pull a squeal from her throat—it felt wonderful to be so close.

Not that he needed to know that. She spun around and gave his arm a swat. "I was supposed to get *you*," she griped.

"Oh, yeah?" Sawyer took a step closer. She could see, by his silhouette against the houselights, that his arms were raised in surrender. "Then go ahead. *Get* me." He stepped closer still, infusing her next breath with that masculine scent of him.

She exhaled, the sound jagged and raw as the tips of his fingers slid down her forearms, further still until he cupped her elbows in his palms.

Her feet were squared solidly below her shoulders, something she paid mind to as his foot slid right in between. She gulped, took one step backward, and met with a wall of sorts. The shed, perhaps? She spun to see a row of barrels nudged up against the shed. *Oh.*

It had started out playful enough, but this…the chemistry blazing between them, this went beyond mere teasing and flirting. This was real, and Betzy knew it.

Years of attraction, on her part at least, coupled with years of wondering where Sawyer's feelings lay. Did he like her more than a friend? She'd been positive that he had, but she couldn't explain why he'd never asked her out. What had he been waiting for—a green light?

Could she give him the green light now?

Too late. She was already leaning into his chest, soaking in his warmth and his smell. She'd dreamt of being in his arms more times than she could count. And now, among the stars, the moon, and the crickets in the night, that dream was coming to life.

As if reading her very thoughts, Sawyer moved his hands to her hips and squeezed. A deep thrill rippled through her at the sensation of his grip. He always was taller than her—now six feet to her mere five and half—but he rectified that by hoisting her up and onto the surface of one of the barrels.

He stepped in to close the gap, one leg sliding between hers, his warm hands still pleasantly on her waist. He came in then, tentatively at first, and brushed his lips against hers like a whisper.

Yes. So good.

If a green light is what he needed, a green light is what he'd get. She wanted more of Sawyer's kiss. Needed it.

Without another thought, Betzy moved her hands up his solid arms, slowly tracing the length of his biceps with her fingertips.

Goosebumps rose over his skin as she reached his shoulders. And then his neck. She cradled the back of his head as his mouth grazed the spot just beneath her earlobe.

"Betzy," he said, voice low and raspy, the heat of his breath a tease of its own.

And then his mouth was on hers once more. A full, strong,

and glorious kiss. A playful push here, a gentle, encouraging pull there, the rhythm like a well-crafted song, the slow and steady build toward that perfect crescendo.

Sawyer liked her. He really did. And while she wasn't sure what that meant, one thing was very certain: now, more than ever, Sawyer Kingsley owned a piece of her heart. She just wondered, with him heading to the other side of the country, if she'd ever get it back.

CHAPTER 2

resent Day

A classical version of Jingle Bells floated into the oversized dressing room as Betzy waited to try on the next wedding gown for Grandma's catalog. This one, an Italian vintage design. Long in the sleeves, low in the back, and tight in the bodice.

Rachel prepped the dress for her by untying the ribbon binding along the back. "Lo did a great job with this shipment. I can't wait to photograph this one and get it on the website. I bet Camila would have picked it if we'd have had it in."

Betzy gazed at the unique beadwork along the neckline, bodice, and sleeves. "She might have," she agreed. "But I love the one she picked. In fact, I loved everything about their wedding day. I wonder if that's normal. Is that how you felt when your brother got married?"

Rachel pulled at the sides of the dress, hunching to create a complete hole for Betzy to step into. "I'm sure it *would* have been if I liked his wife. Camila's amazing. That's why it was so great for you guys."

"True," Betzy agreed. Camila, James' new wife, was easygoing, generous, and a little feisty as well. The perfect match for her younger brother.

Betzy sighed as she thought over the last few months. Attending that wedding, witnessing the magic of their love, it fanned that deep fear within her. One that had been there for years.

Sure, she got to slip into wedding gowns at her grandmother's boutique each time a shipment her size came in, but that was just for the online catalog. The truth was, Betzy feared that her *own* wedding day might never come.

After all, how often had Mom told her *not* to pursue a big career? How many times had the woman drilled it into her head: *Men don't want a woman more successful than them. Just play the part of happy heiress unless you want to wind up a lonely old spinster.*

Betzy hadn't taken the woman's advice, but what if Mom was right?

She pushed the thought aside and tried focusing on the task at hand. "I swear, if my Grandma Lo didn't have me doing this for her, I would have probably said goodbye to my waistline a long time ago." She tiptoed over the mounding silk fabric, setting her feet carefully onto the spot of floor visible in the center.

Rachel wasted no time pulling the dress up around her frame. "Turn," she said, gripping her hips and giving her a spin. At once, she was tightening the bodice, one hefty cinch after the next. "This is going to look incredible on you."

"I heard that," Grandma Lo said from the other side of the door. "I can't wait to see."

The song changed to a modern holiday tune. One Betzy recognized but could never name. "I can't believe it's already December," she said. "This year has flown by."

"Wait until you're my age," Grandma hollered. "When you get to be in your seventies, one year is a mere *point-seven* percent of the life you've already lived. They go by very quickly at that rate."

Grandma had overcome a lot in her seventy plus years. Some might think that a billionaire's life was charmed, but Lorraine Benton had buried her husband, her only son, and one of her grandsons too. Proving that life, no matter financial rank, had its challenges.

"Okay," Rachel said while taking her hand. "Step into some heels. Do you see the champagne colored ones there?"

Betzy glanced over the gorgeous heels lined up along the edge of the dressing room. "Yes, those will be perfect." She slipped into one, and then the other while Rachel helped fasten the straps.

Her friend straightened up once she was through, running a gaze up the dress, when a gasp pulled from her throat.

"What?" Betzy asked, patting at the dress as she looked down to inspect it. "Is there a tear or something?"

But Rachel only shook her head. "No," she said, taking a step back. "It's *your* dress."

Betzy furrowed her brow. "What are you talking about? I'm nowhere *near* getting married."

"That's not what I'm saying. I'm saying..." Rachel died off as she spun a slow, complete circle around her. "I'm saying that *this. Is. Your. Dress.*"

The way she emphasized each and every word caused Betzy to turn and face the mirrors. *Whoa.* Rachel wasn't kidding. Betzy had gotten used to giving each gown no more than a second glance. But as she stepped closer to the mirror, eyes set on her reflection, Rachel's words resonated within her.

Of all the dresses she'd modeled for Grandma's bridal boutique, this—with its champagne colored silk, antique pearl accents, and custom stitching—had Betzy imagining her own walk down the aisle.

"Admit it," Rachel said. "You look incredible."

"Open up," Grandma hollered. "I have to see this for myself."

Rachel came up behind her, gathering the silky train into her arms, then came to a stand. "Okay," she said. "Go ahead and step out."

Betzy nodded as she pulled her eyes off the gorgeous sight of the dress. She reached for the door, turned the knob, and gave it a push.

Grandma Lo's posture shifted before Betzy's eyes. Gone was the hip-leaning, arm-folding scrutiny—the gaze that usually led to moments of tucking fabric here or pinning the neckline there. She lifted her arms at either side, palms up as if she might break into a song of praise.

"Heaven and all its angels are shining down on you today," she said in a whisper. "This is a sign. It's your year. Your time has come at last."

All thoughts of the dress hit the floor at Grandma's words. "*A sign?* You *do* know it's December, right? It can't possibly be my year—it's practically over."

Grandma rubbed her hands together as she approached. "I don't mean it *that* way. I mean that, before this time next year, you'll be walking down the aisle with the man of your dreams. Trust me, I have a sense for these things."

"She does have a sense," Rachel agreed.

"Well, if that's the case, why don't you put this on hold for the ninth of *never* since I haven't met a man I'd even want to marry and I don't sense one coming any time soon."

"Really, Betz?" Rachel mumbled. "The ninth of never? That's pathetic."

"Maybe you've met him, maybe you haven't. But that's what makes it fate," Grandma said with a dismissive wave. "It's got timing of its own."

Rachel was already standing behind her tripod. She adjusted its height while squinting across the room. "Turn more toward the window."

Betzy turned, but she kept her gaze on Grandma as a sharp, prickly irritation bubbled within her. "How do you explain fate when everything we do alters our future? It's like you opening up this boutique after the plane crash. You said *we're* in the driver's seat, remember?"

Sure, Betzy's voice was getting tight and her tone had turned high, but this wasn't a nonchalant conversation. In fact, Betzy had made some very important life decisions based on what Grandma said in the crucial months following the tragedy that took both Dad and Grandpa Benton to an early grave.

Grandma merely chuckled under her breath with the shake

of her head. "Oh, we're in the driver's seat, all right. And we map out our course and go on our way and think we have it all planned out, down to the time of arrival. But then fate takes the wheel."

"Okay," Rachel said from behind the lens, "can we save this conversation for another time? We've got a lunch date, remember?"

"That's right," Grandma agreed, her gaze darting to the crystal clock above the entrance. "Let me just fix this…"

Betzy held still as she gently tucked a strand of hair behind her ear. There was no point in reminding Grandma that her face wouldn't be in the pictures—just the dress. She had to primp Betzy just the same.

"Ah, there! Beautiful!" She attended to the dress's train next, laying it just so before hurrying out of the shot, hands squeezed together in delight.

"If you *were* to walk down the aisle anytime soon," Rachel said as she adjusted the lens, "who would you marry?"

An image of Sawyer Kingsley shot to Betzy's mind. Dark hair, perfectly trimmed five o'clock shadow, and hazel eyes that tugged at her heart like nothing else.

A sigh slipped from her lips. "No one."

"Oh, you've got to come up with one or two," Grandma said. "*Definitely* not Marcus Creighton—that jerk."

"Yeah," Betzy agreed firmly. "Not him." A guy who let her rescue his company before publicly taking credit for that rescue wasn't even worth a mention.

Rachel tipped her head past the camera. "Move your hands behind your back now." After Betzy did just that, Rachel sparked up the conversation once more. "I think if you had to

18

pick someone right now it'd be Sawyer. You two have a marriage contract and everything."

Heat filled Betzy's face, but it was nothing compared to the explosion in her chest. That was the problem with keeping the same friend for so long—they knew all your childhood secrets.

"He *is* still single," Rachel continued.

Grandma shuffled closer to Rachel, watching over her shoulder as she worked. "What marriage contract is this?" she asked. "Go down a little lower, will you? Get the reflection of the floors in a few shots."

"It's nothing," Betzy assured. "We were just kids."

"If it really was nothing," Rachel said, "your face wouldn't match the roses Lo had delivered this morning. Sheesh, good thing I'm shooting from the neck down."

Betzy could hardly believe the irony of it all. What were the chances that fate, Sawyer, and stupid Marcus would come up in the same conversation?

Still, if she were being honest, Betzy had always felt as if she and Sawyer were meant to be or *fated*, as Grandma might say. Especially after that kiss.

But then Sawyer left. Five years later, just when Betzy thought he'd return and life would go back to normal, Dad and Grandpa were killed in the plane crash, and life shifted to a new kind of normal.

Mom, who'd always been closer to the boys, went quiet. Retreated to her room for days, sometimes weeks at a time. Grandma had swooped in to pick up the pieces. Forget the fact that she was hurting too.

Amongst it all, Lorraine Benton, after burying her husband and her son, opened the wedding boutique of her dreams. Not to make money—heck, the family had more than they could spend—but to fulfill an inner desire: to be at the place where happiness begins. In essence, she'd taken fate into her own hands.

An act that inspired Betzy to do the same with one bold move. It hadn't gone well.

She mused back on that time in her life while driving to the clubhouse. Outside, shoppers hurried along the bustling sidewalks. Christmas lights hung from the palm trees along the storefronts, reminding the city of Los Angeles that it was Christmastime indeed.

She couldn't help but wonder if Sawyer would come home for the holidays this year. And if he did, would he reach out to her? Try to get together for a drink and catch up?

After flying in for the double funeral, Sawyer veered from the norm and flew his mother out to New York for the holidays instead. Betzy hoped he wouldn't do the same this year.

"Your mother's going to be here, right?" Grandma asked as she retouched her lipstick.

"Yes," Betzy said. "And Camila too."

"Good, good." Grandma tucked her lipstick back into her purse and smoothed a hand over her blonde hair. Mid-seventies as she might be, Lorraine Benton was beautiful as ever.

The women arrived soon enough. Camila sat next to Betzy, Rachel sat on the other side, and Mom plunked beside Grandma with a sigh.

"You're not going to believe what Kellianne just brought me."

Betzy's heart pumped a clumsy beat out of rhythm. Kellianne, as in Sawyer Kingsley's mom. She and her mom had been close since Kellianne started cleaning house for their family years ago. "What was it?"

Mom dug into her bag, pulled out a magazine, and plopped it on the center of the table next to the decorative butterballs and bread bowl.

Betzy's eyes shot to the headline:

Most Eligible Bachelors From East Coast to West.

"Again?" Betzy was the first one to snatch the magazine off the table and pull it to her chest.

"This one's with *Slipper Magazine*," Mom said. "Last time it was *World's Way.*"

Quickly, Betzy flipped page after page, not bothering to look at the index in front.

Advertisement.

Another advertisement.

Portland's Bachelor.

Makeup tips.

Washington's...Tampa's...

Him. Sawyer Kingsley, one of New York City's top real estate moguls, right there in black and white. And what a stunning picture it was.

Betzy steadied her breath; it felt like a jackhammer was going off inside her chest. The photographer had opted for the night-after-a-long-day look. His white, button-up shirt hung open, revealing a generous view of his sculpted pecs and chiseled abs. The ends of a skinny black tie dangled at either side. In the photo on the left, Sawyer looked off in the distance, his squared jaw and furrowed brow giving him a pensive expression.

She knew that expression well. Loved it.

"I can't believe he didn't tell me about this," Betzy mumbled.

"Maybe he's humble," Camila said over her shoulder.

Rachel hovered over the other side. "No one *that* good looking knows humility."

Betzy grinned, partly amused by their dialogue, and partly wistful as she recalled the walking contradiction of Sawyer Kingsley. He played a cocky male as well as the next guy, with his flirtatious ways and bold, charismatic smile, but beneath that, there was a humble quality. An endearing one at that.

Her eyes drifted to the photo on the right. He was looking straight into the lens in that one, running a hand through his hair with a smile that made her heart quiver and ache.

She'd earned a whole lot of those smiles over the years, but that thought only added to the hurt.

How? How after all this time was she not over Sawyer? She'd sent a piece of her heart with him when he left to New York, secretly hoping he'd come back and marry her. But as the years passed, Betzy realized he'd never promised any such thing.

She gulped past a shallow breath, cursing the heated longing deep in her chest. It reminded her of the incident she tried very hard to forget. The one that forced Betzy to snatch that part of her heart back and bury it. Bury it deep like a worm in the ground.

But all too often, her mind became the beak of a bird, piercing through the soil to snatch it up and devour it whole.

Not right now, Betzy. Don't revisit that right now. She wouldn't. What she *would* do is send Mr. hot, sexy bachelor of NYC a text. Just to prove she could. How many women ogling his spread could do that? Not many, ladies. Not many.

She pulled her phone from her purse and tapped out a text to the one and only.

Betzy: *Check out our lunch conversation topic at the clubhouse today.*

She snapped a picture of his magazine spread and hit send.

"Who's that going to?" Camila asked.

Betzy glanced up from her phone to see that Grandma, Rachel, and Mom awaited her answer as well. "It's to him."

Camila gripped hold of her forearm. "You really do *know* this guy?"

Betzy grinned. Her new sister-in-law was the only one at the table who didn't know about their history.

Rachel pulled out the finger quotes. "They're *friends.*"

A grin spread over Camila's face. "Have you ever kissed him?" That question, sweetened by her Spanish accent, rolled off Camila's tongue with far too much ease.

"Camila," Betzy said with a gasp.

"Well," Grandma Lo blurted. "*Have* you?"

Betzy made a quick survey of the table before nodding ever so slightly.

The ladies' chorus of oohs and ahs gained attention from nearby patrons. It was a good thing Rachel wasn't still shooting pictures of her since Betzy was likely red all the way to her toes.

"Hello, lovely ladies," their table host said cheerily. "Have you made your selections yet?"

Slowly, hesitantly, the eyes peeled away from Betzy and shifted to their host. And while they placed the ladies orders one by one, Betzy was replaying that heavenly kiss.

"Mind if I take a little peek at this for myself?" Rachel asked, gripping the corner with her finger and thumb.

Betzy shook her head. "No, go ahead." She watched numbly as Rachel licked a finger and turned the page.

"Maybe I'll snatch up one of these other bachelors for myself," Rachel said under her breath.

"What magazine is that?" Camila asked.

"*Slipper*," Mom answered. "Hey, that reminds me. Don't the Shays run *Slipper Magazine?*"

Betzy resisted an eye-roll. "Yep."

"That's what I thought. Kellianne says the editor went to school with you and Sawyer. What's her name?"

"Daisy," Betzy said. "*Daisy Shay...*" She added emphasis to help Mom recognize the name. Daisy had caused Betzy a whole lot of grief during their school years. Spreading false rumors and going after any guy Betzy took an interest in, namely Sawyer.

"That's right," Mom said as enlightenment lit her eyes. "I guess Daisy personally delivered three copies of the magazine to Kellianne the day the issue came out."

"I bet she did," Betzy said under her breath. Irritation gripped her fast and hard. Seemed as if Daisy still wanted to get her hands on Sawyer. At one point, she'd accomplished that very thing. Was she simply up to her same old tricks?

Betzy's phone buzzed with a reply just as the host made his way to her. Quickly, she ordered the brie cheese wedge with tomato bisque and handed over the menu. A smile crossed her lips as she saw the name on the screen.

Sawyer: *Me, your lunchtime topic? You don't say. I'm flattered.*

Betzy: *Don't be. Half of the party's over the age of fifty.*

Sawyer: *All the more flattering.*

Betzy: *I guess you're right. Have fun sleeping at night knowing that old women find you sexy.*

Sawyer: *I will. But the more important question is this: do YOU find me sexy?*

Heat flared hot in her chest, neck, and face.

"Did he text you back?" Camila asked.

"Yeah," Betzy said. "Here." She tipped the phone so Camila could read the interaction herself.

"He's a flirt," she said with a grin.

"I know." Another text popped up.

Sawyer: *Is that crickets I hear chirping? C'mon, is it that hard to admit you're attracted to me?*

Betzy shook her head. "Incorrigible." It took her a moment to think of a response, but at last, it came to her.

Betzy: *I can admit that all sorts of men are sexy. It doesn't mean they're my type.*

Sawyer: *Women. Always so complicated.*

A deep, happy sigh spilled through her lips as she looked at the screen. She enjoyed this. Would miss it once it was gone. Which it would be once Sawyer got serious with someone. It was probably the only way she'd really know he'd gotten into a relationship.

"Hey, look what's coming in next month's issue," Rachel said, pointing at a spot on the back page. Betzy read it aloud as she went.

"From hard-working bachelorette to wealthy old spinster. Find out which billionaire bachelorettes are destined to hold onto their money while *men* slip through their fingers."

A hush fell over the table.

A sick knot formed in Betzy's stomach as she reread the title. "You are *kidding* me."

She snatched the magazine from Rachel to see it up close and personal. "I bet you anything I'm on that list."

"You're in your twenties," Grandma countered, but that crease along her brow said she was concerned just the same.

"It doesn't say she's *already* a spinster," her mom said, "just that she's destined to *become* one."

Grandma and Mom exchanged a worried glance.

"Who else do we know that works for *Slipper?*" Mom asked. "We need to know if she's on that list."

Betzy turned her eyes on Grandma next. "Anyone? Think."

Grandma gritted her teeth and snatched her phone from her purse. "I'll ask around. Don't you worry, dear. I doubt they would ever put you on a list like that."

Mom locked eyes with Betzy across the table, her lips pursed in concentration. After all of Mom's warnings that Betzy might end up alone if she pursued a career, there wasn't a hint of *I-told-you-so* in her gaze.

Claudia Benton knew how to play that mama bear role as well as the rest of them, especially when it was to protect the family name.

Betzy imagined the humiliation that might come of it—an appearance in an article that said she was destined to be old and all alone. The very fear that had haunted Betzy since she was a little girl.

Grandma and all of her gumption had given her the courage to compete in the business world with the best of the best and make a name for herself, despite her mother's warning.

The trouble was, that warning might just hold true. A knot of burning heat stirred in her gut.

She would definitely be on that list. And she could guess at who's idea it'd been to put her there: Daisy Shay's.

Camila gave her a tap on the arm and leaned in. "Hey, James is heading out of town with Zander later today. Why don't you come over? We'll come up with a plan to combat the article just in case, and you can fill me in on your history with this sexy bachelor. Oh, and of course, we'll eat something amazing."

Camila wasn't just saying that either. As one of LA's finest private chefs, James' new wife turned ordinary meals into something of magic.

"Rachel can come too, if you'd like," she added.

Betzy gave Camila a grin, grateful to finally have a sister at last. "Thank you," she said. "I'd love that." She glanced down at her phone to see if Sawyer had texted anything more. He hadn't, which left his latest words like black dots against the white screen. *Women. Always so complicated.*

But she had to disagree. Sawyer Kingsley—*he* was the complicated one. No matter how many times Betzy had hoped something might happen between them, she'd met with one too many disappointments in that regard.

He was, in a way, untouchable. Sadly, she would likely never kiss those lips again. Unless, Betzy mused wryly, she wanted to kiss the pages of that magazine.

CHAPTER 3

Sawyer rolled his shoulders back as he headed toward the elevator. As it was in the bustling city, the sights, sounds, and excitement were enough to distract a man for days. Too bad Sawyer had become immune.

His mind always found a way to think about Betzy. And right now, he was hyper focused on her latest text.

The elevator dinged, the doors glided open, and Sawyer joined the crowd as they stepped inside. He moved to the back wall, tugged his phone from his pocket, and gave it another glance. *I can admit that all sorts of men are sexy. It doesn't mean they're my type.*

A stream of irritated curses blared through his head as he shoved the device back into his pocket. How much clearer could she be? Why didn't she just come out and say it? *Sure, you've done well for yourself, and you're not bad to look at, but that doesn't make you marriage material.*

Who cared about a stupid magazine article that claimed he

was eligible in some way? That statement couldn't be farther from the truth. Heck, everything he'd done—the success he'd worked so hard to gain—all of it was for her.

No, he might be single. But that didn't mean he was available. Not really.

His phone gave out a quick buzz. *Please be from Betzy.* One look at the text itself said that maybe it was. It asked one simple question, one he'd been waiting for Betzy to ask. But the name attached wasn't hers.

Daisy: *Hey, bachelor. Are you coming home for the holidays?*

He couldn't help but cringe. Though it hadn't been a necessary part of her job, Daisy Shay had made a point to come out to NY when Sawyer met up with the photographer and the reporter too.

Daisy insisted he join her for a drink after the interview. When he'd declined the first two times, stating his schedule wouldn't allow it, she said she'd simply reschedule her flight and stay a while longer. That woman always was persistent, he'd give her that.

Persistent enough to lean into him at the bar and steal a kiss. He shook his head at the recollection. Sure, Daisy was attractive, always had been. But she couldn't hold a candle to Betzy in his eyes.

Sawyer tucked the phone back into his pocket. He wasn't so sure he would fly home now. Maybe he'd fly Mom out to New York again. Only he knew she didn't want that. Mom preferred the moderate temps of California any day of the week. Plus, she didn't want to leave Mario behind, him getting up there in years and all. The mere thought of their scruffy Beagle made

Sawyer long to give him a rubdown and play with those big, floppy ears.

Home. California really was home. So why was Sawyer waiting so long to get back to it?

Once he stepped out of the cramped elevator, he ran a hand along the back of his neck, hoping to press out the knots forming there. Perhaps he should skip the club tonight and call for a massage instead. Ryan would understand. Heck, he was probably already buying drinks for some chick who'd caught his eye. If Sawyer didn't show, Ryan could skip the inevitable step of apologizing for taking off with so-and-so. Or worse, the part where he begged Sawyer to go home with so-and-so's friend. Awkward, since he declined every time.

He simply wasn't in the mood. And here he'd thought that his trip back home this Christmas would be the one. Either he'd been reading the flirtation in her texts wrong, or his mom was slacking on the details of Betzy's dating life. She was his main source, after all.

"Doesn't mean I'm you're type, huh?" he grumbled under his breath. Perhaps he really had done all of this for nothing. Sure, he'd gained a whole lot—hit the million-dollar mark just six months after working beside Ryan as a real estate investor. The man knew what he was doing, after all. And heck, maybe his uncle knew more what he was doing in the women department than Sawyer had given him credit for. Perhaps he'd been holding on to nothing but a fool's dream.

With that thought in mind, Sawyer headed to the club after all.

Betzy tuned in on the warmth of the crackling fire at her feet, centered between Camila and Rachel once again. She hadn't pictured James as the type to buy a massive beanbag, but ever since Camila stepped into his life, he continued to surprise her. One thing could be said about the informal furniture piece—it was perfect for lounging out on a quiet night in.

"So he takes off after you graduate," Camila said, retelling parts of—as Rachel called it—the Sawyer and Betzy saga.

"Right," Betzy said with a nod.

"But not before laying an earth-shattering kiss on you first," she added.

Betzy nodded. "Mm hmm."

"A kiss that ruined her for every other male on the planet, we might add," Rachel chimed while twisting taffy around her finger. "This eggnog taffy is going to be the death of me, by the way." She wiggled the taffy ring off her finger and popped it into her mouth with a moan.

Camila giggled. "Glad you like it."

"This isn't some tactic to make yourself thinner than all the women around you, is it?" Rachel accused.

"Hey, we're women," Camila said. "We like our curves, right?"

Betzy did her best to laugh along, but inwardly, she was ready to move past the next part of her story. And while she dreaded replaying the event that soured her against fate, Betzy could really use some fresh insight from her new sister-in-law. As supportive as Rachel might be, her radical tendencies often tainted her view. Rachel didn't deny it, either.

"So you've stayed close all this time, right?" Camila said. "Like, from a distance, I mean."

Betzy nodded. "Right. We text off and on a few times a week."

Rachel leaned over Betzy's lap and shot a look at Camila. "Don't you think it speaks *volumes* that they don't talk to each other about their love life? Like, ever?"

Betzy had just moved her gaze off Camila to Rachel, but she ping-ponged back to see Camila give her friend a nod. "Yes, I do. To me, that says the feelings are mutual. You *do* have feelings for him still, right?"

The fire seemed to move from the hearth to Betzy's chest. It was a good thing she was used to Rachel and her direct ways, since Camila, as sweet and innocent as she might be, wasn't familiar with the whole beating-around-the-bush approach, which Betzy had grown rather fond of on the topic of Sawyer Kingsley.

"I guess," she admitted. "But here's the problem. And maybe I'm just going to brush over the last ten years a little because nothing really eventful happened during that time until..." Betzy stopped there. These words needed attention. They needed careful orchestrating. They needed—

"Until she caught him making out with some chick in New York," Rachel blurted.

Camila gasped. "You *did*?"

No, those weren't flames in Betzy's chest after all. It felt more like fire pokers. Dozens of smoldering hot stabs right to the heart. Her standard line of defense shot to her lips.

"It's not like we were dating." A humorless laugh came next as she tossed a hand in the air. "Heck, we were *never* dating. Not even when he kissed me." Oh, how she liked saying the words *he kissed me* aloud. He *had* kissed her. Kissed her like he meant it and then some. And Rachel wasn't kidding; it had absolutely destroyed Betzy for other men. The few guys who'd worked their way up to a goodnight kiss had only disappointed. And Marcus—*ick*—he'd been the worst one of all.

"So tell me how all this went down." Camila shifted in the bag until she stared directly at the high-vaulted ceiling. "I'm going to watch it all play out in my mind."

Betzy couldn't help but smile. "Well, he usually comes home every Christmas, right? And some years I see him, some years I don't. Depends on when we head out to the cabin and how long he ends up staying."

Camila nodded. Rachel reached for another piece of taffy.

"Five years ago he flew back here for my dad and grandpa's funerals," she said. "And of course, he came here for Winston's too," Betzy added, remembering the family's most recent funeral—the dark day they'd buried Betzy's younger brother after the tragic overdose.

"Anyway, I guess I should say that I always kind of assumed that Sawyer and I would be together eventually." It felt odd to admit such a thing. With Rachel, someone who'd been there all along, she hadn't needed to say it aloud.

"So he said he'd come back to LA after he was done in New York?" Camila asked.

Betzy nodded. "Kind of. Not for me. But he did say he was going to New York to shadow his uncle, learn the ways of a successful real estate mogul, then come back to California after a few years. He never said how long it would be, but I just figured it would be like five or something.

"Anyway, after the plane crash, life just…started moving in some sort of haze. I started to see things differently. Stuff I thought mattered..." A chill rocked through her as she allowed herself to slip back into that time for a breath.

"They didn't really matter anymore. I'd been redecorating my penthouse, right? I mean, I was obsessed. Every detail had to be perfect right down to the imported Indian fabric for my throw pillows." She shook her head, recalling the appearance of her front room in the pale morning light just moments after she'd gotten word.

"Mom's the one who called. Told me that something had gone wrong with the plane." Both Camila and Rachel knew most of the details. Grandpa Benton had recently gotten his pilot license. He and Betzy's dad had planned a father-son fishing trip to Wyoming. But there'd been a malfunction in the plane. And in a matter of minutes, two of the most important men in her life were gone.

"It threw us all into a tailspin. There was just so much hurt. But there was that moment, you know? When I was sitting in my practically perfect penthouse, waiting for my mom to come with the car, where I started to resent it." The hot pokers were back in her chest, burning a familiar scar into her wounded heart.

Rachel offered comfort by cozying into her, resting her head against her shoulder as she continued.

"I remember staring at that stupid, *stupid* pillow I'd made such a big deal about. It made me wonder what I'd been doing with my life. I wanted to undo the last two hundred hours I'd spent obsessing over that room and spend them with my dad instead. My grandpa too. Just...our whole family while it was still whole, you know?"

Camila sniffed and wiped her face. "Yes." And she really did know. Camila had suffered a whole lot of loss of her own.

"Anyway," Betzy said, dabbing the corners of her eyes, "I guess it caused this *seize the day* type of awakening in me. And seeing Sawyer at the funeral, allowing him to comfort me through the pain, it felt so natural. And it made me miss him in a way I couldn't explain. I was done waiting for him to finish what he'd started in New York. I wanted him to come home."

Camila shifted so she was sitting upright again. She turned to Betzy with wide eyes. "So, did you tell him that?"

"That's where it gets complicated. I decided I'd tell him. In fact, I told myself that I'd tell him when he came back for the holidays. But that was the year he decided to fly his mom to New York and spend Christmas there. Maybe because he'd just been here for the funerals. Maybe his mom really wanted to spend the holidays in New York before he left. I don't know.

"But it felt like our relationship had been shifting a little. I figured he was coming back soon, and it felt like, to me anyway, that we were working our way into a romantic relationship after all this time."

Camila smiled knowingly. "Hmm, how romantic."

Betzy grinned as well. "In some ways, it was. But like Rachel said, we didn't talk about our dating life, so I was just *assuming* he was available, like me. So Christmas passed. His mom came back into town. And then came New Years Eve."

"Oh my gosh," Camila blurted. "This is like a movie."

Betzy couldn't help but be amused by Camila's excitement. "If it is, this is the scene that makes you cringe, trust me." She put her mind back on that day. The hustle and bustle of getting onto the jet. Making arrangements for a driver when she got into the city.

"I flew out to New York on New Years Eve. We'd been texting back and forth, and I'd asked him what he had planned for the night. He told me he planned to order pizza, kick back on his leather recliner with a drink, and countdown the New Year with the big screen."

Rachel chuckled under her breath. "Such a guy thing to do."

"Next comes the cringe part," Betzy warned. "And mind you, this was me taking fate into my own hands. Seizing the day. Following my heart. Whatever you want to call it, I was doing it, and it felt *right*." The truth of that statement made her heart ache anew.

"I was texting him while the driver took me to his apartment. They'd started blocking off some of the streets for that night's celebrations, but there was still a while to go before the countdown. Anyway, he told me he was heading back to his place, so I watched for him from the car, and didn't get out until he went in.

"I got through security easily enough by showing the doorman my ID, but as soon as I stepped past the security guards, I caught a view of the glass elevator. I spotted Sawyer a split second before some woman took his face in her hands and planted a kiss on him."

Camila gasped. Then groaned. "No...that's not how that was supposed to go."

"Tell me about it," Betzy said. "That was going to be our moment. Our *I secretly love you and I hope you love me too so let's spend the rest of our lives together* moment."

"Those moments don't really exist," Rachel grumbled.

"Oh, they do," Camila said. "Sometimes they just take time."

Betzy shook her head, musing. Her belief was caught between that of the women by her side. "I think they exist. But maybe they don't exist for everyone. Maybe some of us just have to settle for...the Marcus Creightons of the world."

Now it was Rachel's turn to let out a groan.

"That's the guy you dated a while back?" Camila asked.

Betzy nodded.

"James told me about him."

"Yep. That was another mistake. But back then I was thinking it was meant to be, the way we hit it off when we first met. The way I was able to help him save his company. Until he took credit for that himself and pretty much dumped me before I could dump him.

"So now I'm kind of over this idea of fate. And which one is it, anyway? You're supposed to take fate into your own hands? Okay, I tried that. It was a nightmare. I was flying across the country in tears as the New Year came in. And if it's *waiting* for fate to play out, don't you think I've done that too? I mean, how long do I have to wait? Long enough to get on *Slipper's* bound-to-be-spinsters list?"

"I forgot about that," Rachel said, shifting to sit upright beside her. "Did anyone text you back about the article?"

Betzy shot a gaze across the room. She'd left her phone tucked into her handbag the entire evening. "I have no idea."

"Let's find out," Camila said as she climbed off the beanbag. Betzy did the same and, with the two girls at her heels, hurried over to the handbag.

Camila held up a hand as they huddled around the device.

"Now remember. If you're on there, you're going to take the high road."

Betzy nodded. They'd spent the first hour of the evening listing out all the ways she could do that very thing. "Right," she agreed. "I'll find platforms to talk about how outdated and cruel that term is. I'll show the numbers we found about how the typical marrying age is on the rise. I'll get onto talk shows, daytime news, whatever it takes."

The nodding was mutual, so Betzy swiped the screen to see that she had, in fact, received a text regarding the matter.

Grandma Lo: *A friend of mine has a friend whose son works for Slipper. He confirmed that you are listed in that article, Hon, and from what he says, it isn't pretty. Time to gear up our defense.*

"That witch!" Rachel growled. Only she might not have actually said witch.

Knots of anger tangled and twisted in Betzy's gut. "I'm twenty-eight years old."

"Yes," Camila said, "but the article said they'd name women who'd eventually become spinsters. Like they'd ever be able to tell."

Rachel shook her head. "It's probably based on stupid statistics of other billionaire women. I'm sure a lot of them *are* alone since men would probably come in, mess everything up, and spend all their money until they were broke."

"Right," Betzy said with a nod. Only she hadn't paid attention to Rachel's words. She was too busy mentally seeking a different route from the one she'd chosen to take.

Who wanted to step onto talk shows and news shows and face the humiliation of explaining why there was possibly a man out there who would actually be willing to marry her one day? One who was interested in her and not her money.

"I hate Daisy," she spat, looking from one girl to the next. "I'm sorry, and I know I'm not supposed to say that about another human being—"

"Yes, you are," Rachel blurted. "When they're as evil as her, you can hate them."

Betzy regretted saying it already. "I wish I was just…engaged already."

Camila gasped. "To Sawyer!" She screamed his name like it was a solution. "That's it!"

"Oh my gosh!" Rachel started jumping up and down. Camila joined in. "That's it, that's it. Just tell everyone that you're engaged to Sawyer."

If Betzy's eyes could jump out of her face from shock alone, they would. It felt as if they might. "That is *not. Even. Possible.*"

"You said he usually comes back for the holidays," Camila said. And *she* was the sensible one.

"It's not *normal*," Betzy said.

"He'll totally go along with it," Rachel assured. "Sawyer would do anything for you."

Nausea rolled through Betzy's stomach at the mere idea of asking such a huge and ridiculous, not to mention embarrassing, favor. "I would never *ever* ask."

The two women squealed in unison, paying no mind to Betzy's words. "They could stage this amazing proposal at some public place," Camila said. "Oh, maybe your Christmas special of The Lion's Den."

"Yes," Rachael blurted. "And it has to go public like the night before the magazine comes out, so it makes the editor of *Slipper Magazine* look like a total idiot!"

Betzy considered, for just a blink, what that would be like. The Lion's Den, the family's TV show designed to rescue multi-million dollar companies, *was* airing a live special this year...

"No," Betzy said before the stirs in her chest became something more. Revenge was *not* a good motivator. But what was? Dwelling on the fact that they just might be right about her? Wasn't she entitled to a tiny bit of revenge?

She pictured the kiss she'd seen in the elevator. The pain that seared through her at the sight. She couldn't take another letdown. And if she dared ask Sawyer about something like this, she'd probably find out just what was happening in *his* love life. And she wasn't sure she could take that.

"Guys," she blurted. "The high road, remember?"

The chatter died down. The excitement, like a live force in the room, dropped too. Nose-dived was more like it.

"Right," Camila said with a sigh. "No, no, you're right. The other way is better. Let's stick to Plan A."

"I like Plan B better," Rachel said with a *humph.*

Betzy went over the list they'd made in her mind. "I'll reach out, see when I can make a few appearances, and we'll combat this ugliness with grace, the way Grandma Lo would."

"And finesse," Camila added as she snatched the champagne off the counter. She poured a bit of the sparkling drink into the glasses nearby, handed one to both Betzy and Rachel in turn, and lifted her own glass toward the center. "Here's to doing this with grace and finesse."

"With grace and finesse," they repeated. "Cheers."

CHAPTER 4

*S*awyer stepped on the clutch, shifted into fifth gear, and relished the feel of the salty coastal breeze on his face. Boy, did he miss driving in LA. The bright sunlight, gorgeous palm trees, and the open road. This baby, a Lamborghini Veneno, made it all the better. The fact was, Sawyer kept two of his three cars back in LA; no point having them in New York, where he rarely drove.

He'd taken a detour on his way from the private airport, driving past the Benton's estate, where he'd lived a good portion of his life. Betzy had recently purchased a home of her own not too far from the family's estate. He found himself picturing a different scenario where the two met. Where she didn't know him as the close friend whose mom cleaned her home when she was young.

On most days, Sawyer felt as if he'd achieved enough to be worthy of a girl like her. Heck, he'd made more than a splash in the industry.

But then the doubts would creep in. Voices that said he'd never measure up. Memories that told him he'd fallen short before.

A vision of his twelve-year-old self came to mind. There he was, boarding a bus, letter in hand, hoping to catch a glimpse of his dad.

After a whole lot of reluctance, Mom had given Sawyer the address so he could send a letter. He lived just a few towns away. What she hadn't expected was for Sawyer to dig into his race car bank, skip school, and catch a bus to go find the guy's house himself.

He'd gotten answers to all of his questions over the years. At least the ones Mom could answer.

"*Does my dad know about me?*"

"*Yes.*"

"*Does he know when my birthday is?*"

"*Yep.*"

"*Did he ever celebrate one with us?*"

"*No, bud. He didn't stick around long enough.*"

"*Do you think he ever thinks about me?*"

"*Yes, I'm sure he does.*"

"*Then why doesn't he ever come and see me? I bet he'd be surprised to see how tall I am.*"

"*I bet so too.*"

"*Does he like Mario Andretti too? I bet that's where I get it from.*"

"*As a matter of fact, yes. That's exactly where you got it.*"

Mom often wore that same sad smile when answering. Back then, he figured she worried about Sawyer liking his dad more than her. In retrospect, he realized she was worried he'd get his heart broken by a man who wanted nothing to do with him, even if Sawyer was his own flesh and blood.

It grew late before his father pulled into the drive. Good thing he'd told Mom he was going to a friends' house for dinner after school.

He sat behind a large boulder at the corner of the property, waiting as the sun moved closer to the horizon, reflecting on the envelope he'd tucked lovingly into the mailbox. *To Jackson Coller.*

The letter didn't say much. Just that Sawyer wanted to meet him one day. He'd suggested that—since they both liked fast cars—maybe they could go to the Daytona 500 together sometime.

He included a recent school photo, and closed the letter with a few simple words.

It's okay if you don't want to call or come see me right away. Just keep my picture. It has my number and address on it. Hope to see you soon.

Love, your son Sawyer Kingsley.

It was like looking at a movie star or something when he finally pulled up and got out of the car—a shiny black Camaro. It had taken everything in Sawyer not to run up to him and introduce himself right then. Ask to hop in his car and go for a spin.

But he stayed in place, certain that, after getting his letter and seeing his picture and hearing about how much they had in common, his dad would call him. The picture would probably go on the fridge. Or maybe in his wallet. Some parents liked to do that.

He watched, fidgeting with the laces of his high top shoes as the guy—a perfect stranger, really— pulled a stack of mail from the box. Sawyer's letter sat right on top, and it must have gotten his attention too, because he pinned the others beneath his arm to tear it open.

Sawyer watched for his reaction. If it was good, maybe he could come out from his hiding place and let him know he was there.

But as he pulled out the letter, began reading it with narrowed eyes, deep, angry-looking lines creased his forehead. He flipped the letter over to look at the back, which was blank, before tugging the small wallet-sized photo from the envelope.

He shook his head as he scrutinized it. Back and forth while the lines in his face grew deeper. Suddenly, a voice called out from the porch. A woman stood there. Tall with blond hair in a pink dress.

"Jackson?"

The man—his father, he'd reminded himself—darted a look over his shoulder and sandwiched the letter between his palms. "Yep?"

"Did you pick up the groceries?"

At once he crumpled the letter in his hands, along with the picture, the envelope, all of it. "Yeah, they're in the trunk," he mumbled.

Sawyer held very still, eyes set on the man's fist as he marched over to the curb, lifted the lid of a large trashcan, and dropped the crinkled wad right inside.

Not the best day of his life, that was sure. A familiar ache sank into Sawyer's chest at the recollection even still, but it was nothing compared to the pain he'd felt back then.

All from a rejection so dark he hadn't fully recovered. One that left him asking why he'd ever tried. Had he left the situation alone, not reached out to contact the man like he had, Sawyer could have told himself that perhaps his father really did care. That he was out there somewhere hoping to meet him one day.

But it was too late for that.

Driving into the city always did spark up the unpleasant memory, but Sawyer didn't let himself think on it for long. He pulled his mind back to the present as he approached the house in Lake Sherwood.

After a ridiculous amount of convincing, his stubborn mom had agreed to let him help her rebuild the home on the property of her dreams.

Mom had bought the place all on her own, a lakeside house, no less. It just needed more improvement than she'd anticipated. He'd added a few perks for himself as well. A dock leading to the lake. A garage that held his speed boat and water toys, not to mention his third car—the Porsche. He'd drive that back to LA and keep *it* at the storage garage by the airport this time around.

Tall trees lined the property, giving the home an added level of privacy. Sawyer turned his music down as he pulled into the long, narrow drive, eyeing the massive wrap-around porch for any signs of Mom. A smile pulled at his lips as he saw her hovered over a hanging plant, a watering can in hand. She paused to wave at him.

Sawyer waved back and set his eyes on the stairs, waiting for Mario to enter the scene with his flopping tongue and flapping ears. A sliver of fear struck him in the pause. It wasn't like the beagle to miss out on his homecoming. Perhaps the old dog was inside sleeping.

He parked the car, climbed out, and popped the small trunk to grab his bag. "Where's Mario?" he hollered.

His mom reached into the potted flowers, pulling a few dead leaves out of the bunch and letting them drift to the ground. "He's out here. Just curled up by the rocking chair. Give him a holler. He can't hear so well anymore."

A sigh of relief pushed through Sawyer as he hiked the bag over one shoulder. "Mario, boy." He whistled. "Come here, boy. I'm home."

At last, the little guy appeared at the top of the stairwell, tail wagging as he gave out a lone bark. He lumbered down a few steps, meeting Sawyer halfway before hefting back up to keep even with him.

"Hi there, my boy." Sawyer dropped his bag at the top of the stairs and reached out to rub both sides of his soft, furry neck beneath his collar. The dog's velvety ears skittered over the back of his hands as he moved. "That's my good boy." He kissed the little guy on the head, then picked him up and carried him like a football into the house as Mom opened the screen door.

"I'm chopped liver compared to Mario, huh, Mr. New York's Most Eligible Bachelor?"

Sawyer chuckled as he flung his bag to the couch. "Never, Ma." He wrapped his arm around her and pulled her in for a hug. "I'm just not used to seeing this guy so mellow." He wasn't sure why his emotions were so close to the surface. The dog wasn't the *only* one aging. Just how much longer could Sawyer stay away?

Heaven knew he'd made enough arrangements in the LA

area to match his success on the east coast. But the most crucial part of his plan was still missing.

The savory aroma of Mom's cooking became evident in his next breath. "Smells good," he said.

Mom grinned. "Made some creamy potato soup, fresh dinner rolls, and some fudge brownies for dessert."

"Sounds great." Sawyer followed his mom through the dining area and into the kitchen. They caught up on a few things while Sawyer helped Mom set the table in the sunroom overlooking the water. The lake was serene today, a sheet of glass reflecting the nearby trees and all their beauty.

"So, do you have plans to visit any of your old friends?" Mom asked as she dipped a roll into her soup. Sawyer knew who she had in mind. He'd been asking himself that very question for the last six months.

"I'm not sure," he said.

Mom looked down at her bowl and shrugged. "May as well. You're here."

Sawyer hadn't realized it earlier, but she looked more youthful. She was young for a parent of someone his age. And she'd been told she'd pass as his sister over his mother any day.

"You're supposed to look older each year," he said, "not younger. You doing something different?"

She primped her hair a bit. "Oh, I had them put more golden tones in my hair, like I did when I was younger. Of course, I'm doing Botox. Going to the gym more often now that I'm not working so many hours."

Sawyer had always wondered when or if his mom would ever start dating again. If he didn't know better, he'd guess maybe she was. "Huh," he finally said, determined to revisit the topic later. "That's one of the perks of working for yourself. I'm proud of what you've built up over the years with your business, Ma."

She grinned. "Thanks. Training housemaids and keeping track of their schedule beats cleaning house any day."

"I bet it does." He often thought back on all the hard work she'd done, cleaning houses, starting her own business, and raising him all on his own. He'd listed those very things in a card while gifting her a cherry red Dodge Challenger, AKA the car of her dreams, on Mother's Day. He'd known she'd need a list of reasons she should accept the car. Thankfully, it had worked.

Just then his watch buzzed, letting him know he'd received a text. He'd left the connected phone in his bedroom upstairs, but one glance at the watch told him it was from Betzy.

Mom must have seen it too, because suddenly she said something that was very unlike her. "Do you want to go get that? I don't mind."

Had it been from anyone else, the text would be easy enough to delay. As it was, Sawyer was dying to see what Betzy had to say.

"Okay," he said with a nod. "I'll bring out some more iced tea if you'd like too."

"That'd be great. Thanks, son."

Sawyer hurried through the house, up the stairs, and into the room where his phone laid on the bedside table. It buzzed a second time as he secured the device and swiped the screen.

Betzy: *Just curious, are you coming home for the holidays?*

Sawyer: *Who's asking? Is this an admirer?* He smiled as he waited for her response.

Betzy: *Definitely.*

Warmth stirred low in his belly. It was that same baited hook she lured him with every time.

Sawyer: *What kind of admirer are you? Semi-interested or scary-interested?*

Betzy: *Somewhere in between.*

Sawyer: *What I'm asking is, will I be needing a bodyguard?*

When her reply didn't come right away, he hurried down the stairs, snatched the jar of iced tea off the counter, and headed back to the table. A quick look at Mom said she was on her phone too.

"Sorry," he said. "I'm going back and forth with Betzy." It was a cheap trick throwing her name out there, but since Mom liked Betzy, he knew she'd forgive him.

"No problem," she said, tapping on her screen with a grin. She set it facedown on the table, but it took a moment for her to shift her gaze away from it.

She's dating someone. It wasn't just a question in his head. It was more of a realization.

His own phone buzzed, and he glanced down to see her reply.

Betzy: *Sawyer, you're not afraid of me, are you?*

He stared at the screen for a beat. Then he typed out an honest reply.

Sawyer: *Sometimes.*

Betzy: *Then I promise to be gentle. No bodyguard needed.*

More belly heat. Promise to be gentle? And for what? Was she asking him to meet up someplace? Maybe this really would be his year. *Their* year.

"Is that still Betzy you're talking to?" his mom asked from across the table.

"Uh, yeah," he mumbled.

"Tell her hi for me, will you?"

Sawyer glanced up to see that Mom was on her phone again too. The sun was starting to set now. The brilliant tones of red and gold bounced off the surface of the lake. That might be what caused his mother's face to blush. But he was pretty sure it had more to do with whomever she was texting.

"Why don't you tell…the guy you're texting right now *hi* from me too."

She shot him a look with wide eyes, and then her face softened. "It's Ted. You know the guy who owns the gym?"

If Sawyer were honest, he was only halfway invested in the conversation. Voices were screaming someplace in his head that he might just be going on a date with Betzy in the next week or so. "Ted?" he repeated. "From the gym?"

"Yeah," she said, setting her phone down once more. "We're kind of dating, I guess you'd say. I kept meaning to tell you but I worried I might jinx it."

"That's nice," he said with a nod. "He must be something special if he managed to pull you back into the dating world after all this time."

"He's pretty great," she said with a smile. "Did you let Daisy know when you were coming into town?"

"Not yet."

"I'm just asking because she stopped by the house to personally deliver a few copies of your magazine. She was asking, but I told her I wasn't sure."

He let out a sigh. "Thank you."

She grinned. "Go ahead and answer Betzy. Then we'll leave our phones alone until we're done eating."

"Sounds good." But an idea was forming in his mind. An admittedly juvenile idea to make Betzy a little more anxious to get together. She never had liked Daisy very much. Especially when he'd been dating her back in high school.

Sawyer: *You know, Daisy's been asking to get together as well. What do you think—bodyguard or no bodyguard for that one?*

Dots bounced along his screen, letting him know she was tapping out a reply right then.

Betzy: *Definitely get a bodyguard for that one. But don't worry, I volunteer for the job. Free of charge.*

Sawyer covered a laugh. He missed this. Missed goading Betzy into comments like that. Missed the idea of seeing her at a moment's notice. Soon he'd write her back, set up a time to get together.

For now, he'd work on coming up with a plan. Now that he'd made a name for himself. Now that he was ready to come home and pursue the life he'd really dreamt of. And now that Betzy seemed, at least in some ways, open to the idea, what was the best way to win the heart of Miss Betzy Benton—the girl who'd stolen his heart so long ago?

CHAPTER 5

*B*etzy flung back the covers, plopped into bed, and read back through the texts she and Sawyer exchanged beneath the lamplight's glow.

She'd made it clear that she wanted to get together, so why wasn't he picking up where she left off and planning something? He usually did. At least something simple like meeting up for a drink.

What, now she'd have to be the one to do it?

An ache sank into her heart like a sharp, heavy stone. She'd gotten her hopes up again, hadn't she? No matter how many times Betzy tried to shed the idea that she and Sawyer were somehow written in the stars, her rubber band hope would spring right back into place with a resilient snap.

He's still single. There's still hope. Maybe he's waiting for you too. Maybe he, like you, compared every kiss he's had with the one he shared with you. Even the kiss you saw back on New Year's Day.

The truth was, today had been filled with triggers. Triggers that pushed her fear to new limits. Would she really spend the years of her life alone? Her and her money and her cats. She hated cats. And she hated Daisy too.

Stop, Betzy. You dislike her. You don't *hate* her.

But that was just it. Everything seemed to come so easy to girls like Daisy. That girl could flirt with a telephone pole and get it to uproot and step aside for her.

Betzy hadn't been so confident. Sure, in the ways of business she knew exactly what she was doing. She'd been trained well, and had gained plenty of wisdom through experience too. But with men...that was a different story.

Think about it, Betzy, he's not into you. You're like the nerdy little girl he might have liked back in grade school. And now here he was, getting named one of the country's top bachelors for the second year in a row, and *that's* what he's interested in?

He'd probably just given her some sort of pity kiss before he left. It might not have reflected his feelings at all.

The fear grew heavier in her chest. Pushing, swelling, aching. Betzy tried to inhale a calming breath, but parts of that pointed headline popped into her mind, spiking her pulse instead. *Women destined to hold onto their money while men slip through their fingers.*

Betzy could guess at a few reasons wealthy women wound up alone, but that didn't mean they applied to her.

A groan sounded low in her throat as Betzy sank deeper into the pillows. She'd only barely just set her phone down, but already it was buzzing anew.

Please be Sawyer.

The inward plea was silenced as Betzy saw it was Grandma calling.

KIMBERLY KREY

"Hello?" Her attempt to put cheer into her voice failed.

"How are you doing, Hon?" Leave it to Grandma to know how much Betzy needed a kind voice.

"Crappy."

"I know. I'm sorry. We've got you lined up for *five* live appearances over the week following the *Slipper's* release."

Betzy plunked the side of her face into her pillow and sighed. "That's good," she said through smooshed lips. "Guess that's how I get to spend my Christmas break. *Really* great."

"Sweetie?"

"Mm hmm?" The hot sting of tears pricked the corners of her eyes.

"Is something else bothering you?"

Yes, she wanted to say. *I'm worried that I'll be alone for the rest of my life. That I've been waiting for Sawyer this whole time and he doesn't even want me. I'm worried that I missed my chance. I'm scared that maybe there never really was a chance. I worry that my mom was right all along.*

She sniffed. "I'm fine. Just tired."

"Yeah," Grandma said. "It's been a long day. You know, if your dad were here, he'd march right into *Slipper* headquarters and demand they remove your name from that article." She laughed, and Betzy did too.

"You're right." Tears dripped down her temple and onto the sheet. Mom might have bonded best with her brothers, but Betzy was a Daddy's girl all the way. And even though it'd been close to six years now, she hadn't stopped missing him.

"I have one more possible contact at the magazine," Grandma said. "They're working to get a snapshot of the actual spread."

54

Betzy sprung up like a jack in the box. "Of the spinster article? We might be able to see it before it comes out?"

"Maybe," she said. "It's sticky. This source—whomever it is— would be risking a lot. Not just their job, but there's liability too. *Slipper Magazine* could slap them with a hefty lawsuit for leaking information."

Betzy nodded, imagining how nice it would be to know exactly what to expect. Nausea accompanied the thoughts, of course. She hated the idea that she'd be forced to defend herself.

But ugliness like that shouldn't be tolerated, and if Betzy was going to be slammed unfairly in some stupid magazine owned by the spiteful little Daisy Shay, she wouldn't lay down and take it.

"Get some sleep, sweetheart, okay? Tomorrow's another day."

"I'll try. Goodnight, Grandma. I love you."

"I love you, too."

Betzy sank back into place, hoping to shut her mind off and get some rest.

But sleep didn't come easy. At one a.m. she woke from a horrible dream where she'd lost control on live TV and slapped Daisy right across the face. It hadn't seemed so impossible, if she thought about it. Heck, her brother, James, who was as well-tempered as they came, lashed out at a contestant during their last live broadcast.

She played word games on her phone to get her mind off of the dream, and finally dozed off somewhere past two, but by three o'clock she was up again, grumbling one defense after the next. *Think I'm destined to be alone my whole life, do you? Maybe you're the one who'll wind up alone, Daisy Shay.*

At four a.m., Betzy pulled up a sleep app and put on some white noise. Maybe that would help drown out the sounds in her head.

It must have, because suddenly it was six o'clock and her alarm was sounding. She tapped the snooze option and lay back in place.

Suddenly her phone let out an odd ding. One she didn't recognize. Betzy snuck an arm from the covers, snatched her phone off the side table, and looked at the screen.

Message from unknown number.

Two options were listed below. *Receive. Reject.*

A furrow creased Betzy's brow. "Hmm." She tapped the receive button, and watched as a text box appeared.

The following message will dissolve in five seconds. Do not attempt to photograph the image or the data in your phone will dissolve as well.

A spark of excitement flared within her as an image appeared. It was the article. The entire spread filled the screen. To the left, the headline matched the teaser she'd read. She scanned her eyes quickly over the traits of the well known, wealthy women who'd never married. And then came the horror on the right half of the open fold. A photo of Betzy filled a quarter of the page. And there, listed beneath, were bullet points. She read aloud in a frantic rush, trying to catch it all, but there was no way.

"Buying a home versus renting a penthouse. Stocking up on sports cars as a ploy to attract men. Preying on men who feel indebted to her. Naming her plants." Her face scrunched up. "Whatever." She'd named one plant and that was when she was dating Marcus and already the poor thing had died.

Quickly, Betzy moved down the next line. "Refusing to give up the wheel. Refusing to give it up in *bed?*"

A heated gasp tore from her throat. Already the sight was disintegrating before her very eyes. She tried piecing the pixels of the next line together as they grew dimmer, dimmer, gone.

The screen went black.

That was it. Someone had done her a favor. Anonymously given her a peek of the horrible article, and it was so much worse than she'd imagined.

"That witch!" Only that might not have been what she said. The notebook in her bedside drawer became her canvas. In a frantic rush, Betzy sketched out everything she recalled in the layout, scribbling in words that stood out to her as well.

She stared at the page with her sleep-deprived eyes while everything in her mind shifted. Goodbye, high road. Hello, desperate measures. Maybe Camila and Rachel were onto something. And heck, even if Sawyer *didn't* feel the same way about Betzy, he *did* care for her. Deeply. She was sure about that.

Slipper would release its next issue just before Christmas, so she didn't have much time to make magic happen.

Betzy tossed the pen and fished for the bright, red sharpie. Next, she flipped the page of her notepad and created a big box in the center of the page.

#1 Ask Sawyer to propose to me.

#2 Plan public appearance to create a buzz

She paused there and stared at the page. A flicker of reservation pierced through her resolve. Grandma was like a walking lie detector. And never, in a million years, would she go along with something like this. Betzy scribbled the next item on the list.

#3 Convince Grandma Lo that it's real.

But how? They'd have to spend some time with her. Enough to really convince her they were in love.

"The cabin," Betzy blurted as it came to her. "I'll take him on the family trip." She added that to the list.

#4 Take Sawyer to the cabin.

#5 Sawyer proposes the day before the issue releases.

She stopped again. This had to be big. Very big.

Camila had mentioned the Christmas edition of the Lion's Den. That might just be the perfect place.

#6 Flaunt diamond ring in Daisy's miserable face as she shrinks away in shame.

#7 Sawyer goes back to NY. We keep up the charade through the winter and have a fake breakup in the spring.

Shoulders easing just a little, Betzy reread the steps. "There. Start this off right with a plan of attack, just like any successful venture."

The adrenaline pulsing through her could fuel a jet plane across the country and back. But something about it felt good. Better than the despair she'd been swimming in for who knew how long?

She snatched her phone, pulled up Sawyer's number, and sent him a text. Betzy would take things into her own hands once more. Only this time she wouldn't feel vulnerable or exposed, desperate to have him like her in return or at least let her down easy if he didn't.

Now, Betzy felt safe. If he said no, he'd only be rejecting the plan, not her. But she didn't think he'd reject it. She only needed him to *pretend* to like her.

He could do that. And for whatever reason, she felt very sure that he would.

Still, in case he didn't... Betzy snatched the sharpie once more, tore off the lid, and added one small detail along the bottom of the page. *Get someone else if Sawyer says no.*

CHAPTER 6

Sawyer wiped the sleep from his eyes as his phone dinged from the side table.

With a wide yawn, he stretched an arm beyond the warmth of the covers, grabbed the device, and tried to focus on the screen through squinted eyes. The name on top had him seeing clearly in a blink.

Betzy: *I really need to talk to you. Mind meeting me at the clubhouse today?*

He might have been half-asleep two seconds ago, but Betzy's text was a double shot of espresso. She didn't have to specify which clubhouse. In LA, the place to be was the Benton Brother's Clubhouse.

Sawyer: *I don't mind at all.*

Understatement. His phone dinged again.

Betzy: *Great. 12:00 lunch in private cabana #3. See you then?*

Sawyer typed out a reply. *You said private. Does that mean clothes are optional?*

Betzy: *You can come however you'd like. Just don't expect me to be naked.*

Hmm. She didn't take the bait. Normally, Betzy was more... flirtatious. He was just playing after all.

Sawyer: *Fine. Then don't expect me to be naked either. I'll be the one in the turtleneck.*

He waited for her reply. Maybe a laugh-cry face or an LOL.

Nothing.

A dose of irritation pushed through him. He shoved off the blankets, flipped onto his back, and stared up at the ceiling. What exactly did Betzy have in mind—some sort of business venture?

He hoped not.

A tap came to his door.

"Come in," he hollered.

The door creaked open, and his mom peeked in.

"Hey, you. How'd you sleep?"

"Awesome," he said. "I'm not used to hearing crickets at night. I love it."

She grinned. "Want to come to the gym with me?"

It was that moment Sawyer remembered that Mom was dating someone. "Will *Ted* be there?" he asked, lifting his head off the pillow.

Mom held his gaze for a blink, then grinned. "Yes..."

"Can I arm wrestle him? If he loses, he can't date you."

"He won't lose."

"Tsk." Sawyer shook his head. "I'm buff, Mom." He flexed to prove it.

"Yeah, but he owns the gym. And he lifts, like, ten times a day."

"You're dating a meat head?"

At once she hurried into the room toward the bench at the foot of the bed. He wasn't sure why until she picked up a throw pillow and tossed it at him.

"Mom..." he said, shielding his face.

"Take it back," she said with a laugh, "or I'll throw another one at you." Sawyer put his hand down, prepared to amend his statement when a black and white pillow slammed right into his nose.

"Ma! When did you become so violent?"

She was laughing now. And tossing more pillows too. " He's not a meat head. Make the bed behind you, will you? There's oatmeal on the stove if you'd like some."

"So you're leaving without me?"

She stopped at the doorway and spun around. "You *do* want to come?"

Sawyer pictured running through the neighborhood. The fresh breeze, uncrowded walkways, and air that smelled...like home. "I think I'll go running today instead. And do squats. And lift those barrels in the backyard over my head and grunt like a gladiator."

"Okay," she said. "You going to see Betzy today?"

Anticipation revved within him. "Yep. She asked me to show up at the clubhouse naked, but I told her I didn't think that was appropriate."

"Ah. Right."

"I'll let you know how it goes."

"Okay. Maybe we can do dinner sometime this week here at the house. You bring Betzy. I'll bring Ted?"

HER BEST FRIEND FAKE FIANCÉ: BENTON BILLIONAIRE SERIES

Sawyer gulped. "Let me test things out today. I'll let you know."

Mom leaned along the doorframe and sighed. "Well, see you in a while."

"Have a nice workout," he said.

Sawyer wasted no time getting laced up and hitting the streets. Even in the daylight, signs of Christmas were every-where. Holly berry wrapped around street lamps. Porches decorated with antique sleds, fake snowmen, and stuffed Santas. He wondered how Betzy might decorate her front porch. She owned a home of her own now. Did it hold candles and potted chrysanthemums for the season?

She always did have good taste.

Similar musings went through his mind as Sawyer headed to the clubhouse. He went early, met Duke there for a round of golf before lunch, and somehow made it through the entire game without telling Duke he was meeting up with his sister.

"Let's do golf again before you take off, man," Duke said while closing his locker door. He eyed his man-bun in the mirror. "Or we can go out for a drink. Pick up on a few chicks..."

Sawyer's gaze shot to a group of men headed toward the other side of the locker room before settling back on Duke. "Yeah. Sounds good."

"When you moving back here anyway? I thought this whole New York thing was supposed to be temporary."

Sawyer tipped his head as he considered that.

"I know Betzy would be happy if you moved back. I think she's secretly hoping that little marriage contract you guys put together holds firm."

The laugh Sawyer managed came out forced, but that's only because there were fireworks going off in his chest. A premature celebration at Duke's words.

"You think so?"

Duke rolled his neck. "Totally."

"Hmm..."

A buzzing sounded, and Duke put up a hand as he reached into his pocket. "I better get that. I'll be in touch."

"Sounds good." Sawyer hadn't wanted to get his hopes up, but it was too late for that now. What if, in some roundabout way, Betzy actually wanted to discuss that contract? He could hear it now: *Remember that little arrangement we drew up twenty years back? Well, you're twenty-eight, I'm twenty-eight, and we're both still single...*

Calm down, man. Sawyer glanced at his watch, realized he had time to swing by the gift shop if he hurried. Maybe he'd show up wearing that turtleneck after all. It'd been far too long since he'd heard the sound of Betzy's laugh. And there was no better feeling than knowing he was the one who'd earned it.

The clubhouse did not disappoint. Sawyer opted for the men's charcoal turtleneck, the famous crest stitched into the upper right side. *Perfect.*

Another glance at his watch said it was twelve o'clock on the dot. Quickly, he made his way toward the cabanas, flashing his membership card as he checked in. Soon he'd know exactly what Betzy had on her mind. If it wasn't what he hoped it would be—and he should face it now, it probably wasn't—he'd be disappointed. But either way, Sawyer knew this was the year to make his move.

Go right ahead, came that inner voice. *Get ready for rejection.*

It was the same voice that tormented Sawyer year after year. *Still not enough money. Still not enough success. Still not enough to score a woman like Betzy Benton.*

After the incident with his father, Sawyer had convinced himself that he'd simply jumped the gun. If he'd have waited until he was a little older, the guy might have been interested in meeting him.

Heck, they could've become friends. Hung out. Grabbed a couple of drinks. Sawyer had spent years scrutinizing the school photo he'd given him. Of *course* he rejected the awkward adolescent in that picture—some freckled kid with big teeth and overgrown hair. Why had Sawyer picked that year to grow it out anyway?

As time passed, he found himself wanting to send the guy a list of his recent accomplishments.

What do you think about these? Am I good enough now?

It was no wonder he'd tortured himself over this whole thing with Betzy.

But now was his time to silence that voice.

No more waiting around as the years ticked by without her. Sawyer had known what he wanted since he was eight years old. This time, he'd make his move, ready or not.

CHAPTER 7

*P*rivate cabana number three offered the quintessential view of serenity. An infinity pool that seemed to go on for miles. Palm trees swaying in the distance. Music strategically selected to allow for a peaceful, quality experience.

But even still, Betzy was anything but calm. Two opposing emotions warred within her as she waited for Sawyer to show. She pulled in a soothing breath and pictured what the next few minutes of her life would look like: *I'm about to ask Sawyer Kingsley to be my fake fiancé.* That fact was enough to twist her nerves into one massive train wreck.

When she let the idea resonate, her palms broke out in sweat, her heart pounded itself into a frenzy, and her throat dried up, which forced her to take yet another sip of her iced tea. Poor Phillip, her cabana attendant, had already refilled it twice.

To counter the unpleasant emotion, Betzy tried to stick with a different focus: Daisy. And poof, the nerves were gone. Magically replaced with something quite different: fury.

But the fury came with a physical backlash all its own—chest tightening, fist squeezing, and jaw clenching until it hurt. And while those weren't great side effects, they came with a tempting promise of something she really wanted—revenge.

Daisy's article would be made irrelevant in one hot media flash. Boom! And there'd be no avoiding it. No pulling the magazines off every grocery store stand and digital shelf. It would be out there for all to see, proof that *Slipper Magazine* wasn't as "slipper-stealthy" as they thought.

That reassurance brought with it an emotion all it's own. Excitement. Betzy could not wait to put Daisy in her place.

"Your guest is here, Ms. Benton."

Betzy spun to glance over her shoulder, but a simple glance wasn't enough. She almost didn't recognize the clubhouse merchandise he sported. Mainly because the twill turtleneck had never *ever* looked so good.

Sawyer's eyes scanned over the LA landscape, wandered across the table, and then settled on her at last.

Holy gorgeousness!

Sure, she'd stared at his bachelor spread at least four dozen times in the last twenty-four hours, but seeing him up close and personal was an experience all its own. One that had become increasingly impressive over the years.

That jaw was chiseled out of god-marble. Was that a thing? And he had the most attractive smolder when he squinted against the sunlight. Those hazel eyes slightly narrowed, making him look so serious.

Betzy came to a stand as he rounded the table, and watched

as his face transformed from that brooding expression to a full and glorious grin. Yep, that killer smile still had the same effect.

A flash of heat flared in her face. Chills rippled up her arms. Heaven help her.

She smiled in return as he came in for a hug. He smelled incredible. A spicy, heavenly scent that reminded her of all of his masculine qualities. The things that had set them apart since they were young.

He was the one to squish the spiders when the eight-legged things got into the house. He'd always been the one to jump into the lake at the cabin to test out the water for her. And best of all, *he'd* been the one to take her by the hips, hoist her onto that barrel, and give her a mind-blowing, life-changing kiss she'd never forget.

"Hi," she said softly. Their embrace was caught between formal and familiar. Each using the same approach: one arm wrapping around the shoulder, the other coming in lower around the waist. But then Sawyer kicked things up a notch (as if she weren't already rattled enough) by rubbing his scruff-covered jaw against her cheek. "It's good to see you." He kissed her cheek, and her pulse spiked into oblivion.

"It's good to see you too," she said. But suddenly, she wasn't so sure that it was. This all seemed so easy for him. Mr. New York's Most Eligible Bachelor. For all she knew, he could be juggling ten girls at once back home. And here she was, unattached, and waiting for him to move back home and decide that he wanted her?

"You look beautiful," Sawyer said as he held the back of her chair; he must have waved off the attendant.

"Thank you." She lowered herself back into the seat.

"I'll be back momentarily with the menus," Phillip announced, stepping back into her line of view with a nod.

"Thank you," Betzy said before shifting her gaze back to Sawyer. "I'm starting to wonder why we didn't have *you* model for the clubhouse catalog. Those turtlenecks would sell like hotcakes, the Los Angeles warmth aside."

Another grin. "You're flattering me again. I like it."

She chuckled, and suddenly the tightness in her muscles relaxed a bit. As much as the chemistry between them put her in knots, Sawyer's easy manner and playful ways made Betzy feel right at home.

"So," Sawyer said, resting his forearms on the table's edge. "What's new?"

Talk about fireballs in her chest. The right-at-homeness took flight. It was a full-on explosion as she considered saying what she'd planned to say. *Keep your emotions out of it. This is business.*

"Well," she said, reaching for her iced tea once more. She'd need a potty break very soon. "I've got a proposal for you."

CHAPTER 8

a proposal.

The word sank like a rock in Sawyer's gut as he took in Betzy and all her beauty. That gorgeous auburn hair accenting her flawless skin. Cheeks that glowed when she smiled. Eyes that let off an unmatched kindness, unique in the world of high society and big money.

"Okay," he encouraged with a nod. "Let's hear it."

"So *you* were featured in *Slipper Magazine*'s November issue. Now, they plan to feature *me* in their next one."

He lifted a brow. If the magazine wanted to feature the most eligible bachelorettes in the LA area, Betzy would definitely be at the top of that list. It made Sawyer feel one giant step further from gaining her affections. How many more men would be in the running?

"But it's not anything like yours," she assured. Her cheeks grew pink as her gaze dropped. Sawyer followed the action, watching as she ran a finger along the linen tablecloth. Back and forth.

"There are a ton of wealthy women out there who never got married," she said, casting him a quick glance before dropping her gaze once more.

Sawyer gave her an encouraging nod, wondering where the confident woman he knew had gone off to.

"Anyway," she continued with a shrug. "The article lists common characteristics of those women, calling them spinsters, which is evil, and then it goes on to show how at least *one* billionaire bachelorette is destined to wind up on that list as well."

A rash of angry heat flared in his chest. "Not *you*," he said, tone low and even.

She looked up. "It is me. I saw it for myself."

Sawyer slapped a hand on the table, causing the glasses to tremble and shake. "That is *rich*." Seemed as if her rivalry with Daisy Shay was worse than he thought. Her family ran the magazine, after all.

"She really has it out for you," he said.

Betzy nodded, her shoulders lifting suddenly. "Right? Can you believe that?"

"No, as a matter of fact, I can't. We've got to do something." Adrenaline raced through him from his shoulders to his toes. He fought the urge to shoot out of the chair and pace.

"That's exactly why I texted you," Betzy said.

Sawyer held her gaze. "What do you have in mind?"

She bit her lip, shut her eyes for a long blink, and shook her head with a laugh. "I can't believe I'm asking you this." She licked her lips next, blew out a pursed breath, and covered her mouth with one hand.

"What is it?" he urged. "Betzy, you know you can ask me anything." Heck, he'd dreamt of slaying dragons for this girl nearly half of his life. She'd just never had any dragons she couldn't slay on her own.

But was that about to change? He leaned further onto the table.

Betzy held his gaze as hints of that dimple appeared in one cheek. "Would you be willing to…"

"To what?" The laugh coating the word bordered on madness.

"To be my fiancé?"

Sawyer gulped.

"Just for show," she added. "In time for the article to come out?"

The choppy delivery of that question made him pause. "You want us to pretend we're getting married?"

"If you don't want to, or you're dating someone, or you'd rather not deal with all of this—"

"Of course."

"Of course, what?"

"Of course, I'll do it," he assured.

" You will? You'll do it?" At once Betzy was off of her seat and circling around to him. Sawyer stood up in time to receive a hug that felt very different from the one he'd gotten a moment ago.

Anticipation buzzed through his blood.

This was his chance.

This was his dragon.

This was his way to win Betzy's heart once and for all. He couldn't help but think back on the conversation he'd over-heard between Betzy and her mom years ago. If the woman hadn't changed her tune yet, perhaps this would help. "We'll make them sorry they ever dared to mess with Betzy Benton," he promised.

Betzy squeezed him tighter before stepping away. "That's right," she cheered. "Oh my gosh, thank you! I can't believe you're actually on board."

As Betzy made her way back to her seat, their attendant entered the cabana once more.

"Your menus," he said. "Press the signal once you're ready to order and I'll be at your service."

"Thank you," Sawyer said with a nod. He rested the menu on the table, figuring they'd order once business was through.

"So, if we're going to do this, we've got to do it right. Do you have a plan?"

A dimple-flashing grin spread over her face. "Absolutely."

There was the Betzy he knew. Confident. Poised. Ready to take on the world. She produced an oversized bag and pulled out a notebook. After a quick glance over her shoulder, Betzy set it on the table for him to see.

Sawyer flinched at the harsh appearance of angry strokes in thick, red ink. He smiled as he read the first item on her list. *#1 Ask Sawyer to propose to me.*

He tapped it with one finger. "Check."

She grinned shyly, the pink returning to her cheeks.

He set his eyes back on the list. The second one mentioned a public appearance. Yes, they'd have to be seen once or twice to make it convincing. And then he got to number three. "Your Grandma Lo isn't in on it?"

Betzy shook her head adamantly. "She'll never approve of it."

Never approve of *it* or never approve of *him?*

"Grandma Lo worries everything will turn into a scandal," Betzy explained.

"But your mom's okay with it?" The question was heavier than Sawyer wanted to admit. A sharp ache grew in his gut as he waited for her reply.

"My mom likes to play dirty. It's what usually sets us apart, but in this case…"

Sawyer tried not to get stuck on her response, but it didn't do much to put his mind at ease. If anything, it seemed they were in a predicament, the whole *desperate times called for desperate measures* type of thing.

Measures as desperate as having your daughter accept a proposal from the housemaid's son. Sure, that housemaid was one of Claudia Benton's closest friends, but that didn't, in the world of known names and big money, make Sawyer a worthy candidate for her daughter.

At once, Duke's offer shot to his mind. "You should probably tell your brothers. I just golfed with Duke. He asked me to go grab some drinks with him, pick up a few chicks while I was here."

Betzy's face scrunched up.

"His words," he assured, "not mine. Anyway, I say we tell our families. If your grandma won't go along with it, we'll work on convincing her."

She nodded. "We won't be able to tell my mom's boyfriend

either. Matthew would never go along with it. But he'll be easy. My grandma will be tougher since the two of us are so close."

She shifted her gaze to look over the view, her gorgeous blue eyes reflecting the pool and sky and all their glory. And for a moment, it hurt to look at her. Hurt with a longing that might never be met. With a passion he might never fulfill. And with a determination to help this woman whether she felt the same or not.

"I think with my grandma…" Betzy said, her brow furrowed in concentration, "we'll have to say that, you know, we've been flirting off and on while you were gone. And that when you came back this time, we had lunch…" She waved a hand toward him. "And just hit it off."

Sawyer managed a smile. "Okay."

"Or," she blurted, "maybe we say that we told each other how we really felt *months* ago, but this is the first time we've been able to, you know, act out on it."

Heat flared low in his belly. "That would probably be more convincing, since I'm going to propose before the month's through."

Betzy laughed. "Right."

"So," he asked. "This is kind of our first semi-public appearance?"

Betzy glanced at the guests spread out on sun chairs below. The others who stood up to the bar having drinks. "Anyone who tried hard enough could see us together up here, so sure," she said with a nod.

"Well, then…" Sawyer reached an arm across the table, rested a hand over hers, and tucked the tips of his fingers beneath her palm. Her skin was warm and silky. And when he glanced up to meet her gaze, the belly heat flared up anew.

She blushed, shifted in her seat, and then nodded to the list. "Are you okay with the rest of that?" Her voice was shaky now.

Sawyer followed her gaze, moving back up the page to find where he'd left off, but a random line scribbled along the bottom caught his eye. *Get someone else if Sawyer says no.*

"Whoa."

She must have followed his gaze because suddenly Betzy was reaching across the table and crossing it out with her pen. "Don't need that," she mumbled.

Hmm. He forced his eyes back up to where he left off. "I'm coming to the cabin with you?"

"You don't have to, of course. But it'd be fun. It's been years since you and your mom came with us. She's invited too, of course. Plus, I think it's our only chance of convincing my grandma. And Mom's boyfriend. *And* if his daughter brings up her kids we'll need to convince them too."

This was starting to sound bigger than Sawyer first realized.

"The cabin is also good because if we disappear together, it will be more convincing that our relationship is real. If we really were dating, that's probably what we'd do, right?"

"Right," he said.

Sawyer could hardly get over the way that sounded on her lips. If they were really dating. If he had it his way, they *would* be. His adrenaline spiked at the sight of number five: *Sawyer proposes...*

How many years had he imagined getting down on one knee for this woman?

Sawyer had to slow his next breath through pursed lips. He

was getting ahead of himself. So far, she'd asked him to do a favor. One step at a time. Number six made him grin.

"Flaunt the ring in Daisy's miserable face as she shrinks away in shame?" he said, lifting a brow at her.

Betzy hurried and crossed out that last part about Daisy shrinking away, but left the flaunting the ring part in place. "You have to understand, I was on the brink of insanity last night." She reached out again and crossed out the entire thing. "There."

He nodded. "I get it."

"Oh, and I'll buy the ring," she chirped. Betzy couldn't have known it, but those words were razor sharp.

He narrowed his gaze. "No."

Her eyes went wide. "Sawyer, you're doing me a favor."

"Money's not an issue for me anymore," he said. "Get used to it." Sure, he'd slapped a little sting on the words, but he couldn't help it. If there was a sore spot between them, *that* was it. He'd worked ten hard years to make sure money wasn't an issue. Wasn't *the* issue between them.

At last Betzy nodded, her eyes dropping back to the notebook. "Fine. You can always return it."

He followed her gaze to the bottom of the page. *Sawyer goes back to NY. We keep up the charade through the winter and have a fake breakup in the spring.*

Yes, he'd known that was coming. She wasn't asking him to actually marry her, for heavens' sake. So why did it feel like he'd been sucker-punched low in the gut?

Because he *was* a sucker. He'd almost had himself convinced that Betzy really did want him. That it would, on some level, be real for them both.

It wouldn't.

The list made that clear enough. She wanted to stick it to Daisy, preserve her image, and move on with her merry little life, free of him. Heck, Betzy was prepared to ask some other guy if Sawyer said no. That said it all, didn't it?

"What's wrong?" Betzy's question was distant, faded compared to the clamor in his mind.

Sawyer forced his gaze back to her and cleared his throat. "Nothing."

She tipped her head, inspecting him with an expression he knew very well. Kindness. Concern. His earlier resolve set in once more. Whether Betzy wanted to be with him or not, he cared about her. Wanted to protect her. And he would, no matter what, slay the dragons that threatened to hurt her.

"Is everything okay? You can totally say no to this if you'd like. I wouldn't blame you."

But Sawyer shook his head and steadied his resolve. "No," he assured. "I want to do this. For you. I'm in."

CHAPTER 9

"A re you sure this is a good idea?" Sawyer's mom asked while stirring a pot of soup. Vegetable beef this time.

"No," he answered. "I think it's kind of a terrible idea," he admitted with a laugh. "Especially since, just a few months ago, the editor of the magazine planted a kiss on me during her trip to New York."

Mom spun around, flicking the spoon out of the pot as she moved. A splatter sounded, and Sawyer spotted splotches of soup on the cabinets.

"Sorry," she said. "But Daisy kissed you when she came to New York?"

He shrugged. "Barely. We were sitting up to the bar. She was a few drinks in, so was I. Then suddenly she leaned over and kissed me." Sawyer wadded up a handful of paper towels and ran them beneath the faucet.

"What did *you* do?"

He wiped up the splotches of soup as he spoke. "I pulled

away pretty quick. I tried to do it gently. I didn't want to hurt her feelings, but I didn't want to encourage her either. She can come on pretty strong."

"So then what?" Mom asked, holding her hand out to take the paper towel wad from him.

He handed it over and watched as she sopped up a few splatters along the stovetop before tossing it in the trash bin.

"I apologized. Told her that my mind was kind of on someone else. I didn't specify, but she guessed it was Betzy."

"You're kidding," Mom said with a gasp.

Sawyer shook his head. "She said something like...I don't know, that Betzy wasn't waiting around for me. That I shouldn't be counting on it."

Mom stirred at the soup once more before abandoning the tall spoon and folding her arms. She squared a look at Sawyer. "Do you think you're the reason she's going after Betzy?"

He shook his head. "No. They've never liked each other. That's all I know."

"Yeah, and they've *both* liked you. *You're* the common denominator." She grabbed hold of the spoon once more and stirred. "I don't think I'll go to the cabin with you guys," she announced.

"Why not?"

"First of all, I was already considering Ted's offer to go skiing with him this week. I figured I'd see if I could bring you along. But this way, you can have that time with Betzy without your *mommy* there."

Sawyer let out a laugh. "Fine."

"How long ago did Daisy go out there?" Mom asked.

Sawyer counted back the months. "August sometime. Maybe the beginning of September."

"When are you and Betzy going to say things started being... romantic between you?" she asked next.

"I guess I can say it was around that time."

"So, three months and then you propose?" she asked.

"Yeah, but after a lifetime of loving her..."

His mom's gaze met his, an almost worried look in her eyes. "You're not going to get hurt, are you? Doing this?"

Sawyer tried to shrug it off, but the heat flaring in his chest made him gulp first. "I might," he admitted. "But I might just be able to show her how good we are together. In case she doesn't already know."

Mom motioned him over, and Sawyer readied himself for one of her long, sappy hugs. Which was exactly what he got once he neared.

"I love you, Sawyer," she said, squeezing him tightly before stepping back to the stovetop where she leaned on one hip. "I'm torn on this one. I care about Betzy, and I'm glad you'll be able to protect her image in time for the article to release. But you've waited a lot of years to make a move on her. Is this really the way you want to go about it?"

"No," he admitted. "But I can't let someone else step in and do it. Besides, it's my own fault for waiting so long. This is what I get, I guess. Should've gone after her sooner."

Mom nodded, her eyes drifting toward the living room where they'd set up the tree together.

"Why didn't you do it sooner?" she asked. "Each year, it seems like you're going to, but then you just...don't."

Sawyer never did tell his mom what he'd witnessed at his

father's that year. For a reason he still couldn't explain, he felt a level of shame over the whole thing. Like he'd gotten what he deserved for ditching school and going out there and...and not being a good enough kid.

"I have my reasons," he finally said.

His mom studied him for a blink before nodding. "Who knows?" she said with a shrug. "Everybody's love story is different, right? Maybe this is where yours starts. This could be the crazy beginning to your own happily ever after."

Sawyer forced a smile to his lips, hoping it didn't look as fake as it felt. "Yeah," he said, "you never know." It was, after all, exactly what he hoped for.

He waited for the idea to replace the tumult happening in his heart. When it didn't, one final warning crept in. *Hold onto your heartstrings, Sawyer. This could be one painful ride.*

CHAPTER 10

*B*etzy eyed the piece of artwork before her. A unique, three-dimensional painting of a tall, puffy-tailed poodle. The artist had used a blend of mediums to create realistic-looking dog hair that popped off the canvas. According to the description beside it, the piece featured the artist's very own dog's collar and charm as well.

Betzy tried very hard to pay attention to details like that—she was supposed to introduce the piece for auction in a few short minutes—but was having a very hard time focusing with the feel of Sawyer Kingsley so close.

Sawyer had been asked to play a part tonight: Serious-boyfriend-who-was-playing-it-down-in-public. So far, he was doing everything right. Staying close by her side, wandering only slightly as he observed one piece or another, only to slip up behind her, so closely she could feel his breath on the back of her neck. A sensation she paused to tune into even then.

So good.

They'd arrived at the event close to two hours ago. Dinner had been served, and the guests were making their way around the banquet room to study the pieces up for auction.

During the banquet, with several high profile people seated at the table, Sawyer would catch her eye and give her an admiring smile or flirtatious wink.

Gestures like those set off Betzy's internal microwave, sending just enough heat through her to warm her cheeks and neck. The interactions, along with her physical response to them, would definitely have guests talking.

If they could see what was happening on the inside though, they'd know how very off-balance this whole thing was. While Sawyer was playing a part for their company, the cameras, and the public eye, Betzy battled feelings she'd had since she was a little girl.

She fought off the sadness that threatened to seep in at the thought. *Just focus on the revenge, Betzy. That's the only thing you can control.*

"Have you studied this piece long enough?" Sawyer's deep, masculine voice sounded from behind. And there he was, stepping things up a bit more by grazing his chin over the top of her bare shoulder, tickling the tender skin there with his short stubble.

A thrill shot through her at his touch.

Holy smokes. If she had any semblance of self-preservation, Betzy would abort this mission right here and now. Heck, she'd be a pile of ruins after this was through. But how could she stop when it all felt so good?

"I'm getting a little jealous of Buster, here," he added with a laugh.

Heart swelling in heated, longing thumps, she turned her head the slightest bit toward him. The action caused his lips to ever-so-slightly graze her jaw. A flash of heat shot to her cheeks.

"It's almost time for you to announce, right?" he asked.

"Right. Are you still okay to walk up there with me and add in a line about Mario?"

Joanne Levia, the elegant woman running the event, had loved the idea when Betzy presented it. Especially since Sawyer, being a dog person, could add his own personal touch to the intro. It didn't hurt that he'd just earned himself yet another Bachelor title.

"Of course," he assured.

Luckily, the auction would stream live, allowing bids to come in from all over the world. The live stream would play a key part in making their public appearance a little more public.

It wouldn't make a giant splash, but it *would* make a very nice ripple, which was exactly what they needed.

Betzy spun to see Sawyer push a hand through his gorgeous dark hair, an action that made her feel a little wobbly on her stilettos.

Suddenly his brow furrowed, and he sunk a hand into his tux pocket. Yes, he looked amazing in that thing. And yes, the single ladies in the building were all abuzz over him. She'd overheard several of those conversations without even trying.

"Oh no," he mumbled while looking at his phone screen. Sawyer's face went pale.

Betzy's heart skipped. "What's wrong?"

"It's Mario. My mom says she's rushing him to the vet."

The vet—right now? Betzy scrambled for the right words.

What were the chances something would go wrong with the poor dog at a moment like this? She shot a look to the platform across the banquet room, wondering how soon the auction would begin.

"It's probably nothing," Sawyer said, seeming to follow her gaze. "We can stay. I'm sure he's fine."

Betzy nodded. "Well, only if you're sure." Relief flooded in, but it fled just as quickly at his next words.

"I *am* kind of worried about my mom though. Mind if I step outside and give her a call?"

She couldn't help but swoon just a little from the concern he had for his mother. "I don't mind at all," Betzy assured. "Go ahead."

Sawyer gave her a conflicted look before moving in to press a kiss to her forehead. "Thank you." And then he was gone, leaving the zips and tingles from his touch to spark over her skin.

If *that* went on live TV, it might cause closer to a splash than a ripple. In her heart though, it was a full-on tidal wave.

She watched until he stepped into the foyer and out of sight. If Kellianne was taking the dog in at this hour, it was probably serious. Plus, they'd had Mario since they were back in high school. He couldn't have too many years left in him. What if the dog was deathly ill? What if this ended up being his final hour, and Sawyer was stuck here doing Betzy an enormous favor?

At once the *what ifs* became too much. She spun in place and spotted Joanne Levia striding past the silent auction board, a champagne glass in one hand.

Betzy hurried over to her and, with a bit of panic in her heart, explained the situation. Luckily, the woman was quick to insist that Betzy excuse herself and join Sawyer in attending to the dog.

"If you don't mind us mentioning that it was a dog emergency that pulled you away, we'll be able to milk it for all its worth," the woman assured.

"No," Betzy said with the shake of her head. "I don't think he'd mind at all. Thank you."

Anxious to get back to her date for the evening, Betzy made her way to the foyer. It took her a moment to spot him, but at last she saw the gorgeous bachelor by a set of potted aspen trees, one arm folded across his chest, the other rubbing a hand along the back of his neck.

She walked around a cluster of female guests, shifted her way through a larger group of loosely scattered men, and finally came up behind him at last. Betzy moved to rest a hand on his shoulder, but thought better of it.

"How's he doing?" she asked from behind.

Sawyer let out a heavy breath. "I'm not sure. They just arrived." The nearby trees were decorated with lights and crystal. She caught the reflection of it in his hypnotic, hazel eyes. "I guess Ted drove because she was too upset."

"Ted?" Betzy asked.

He shot her a half-smile. "Her new boyfriend, apparently."

She couldn't hold back the brow lift. "Oh? That's awesome. My mom's been getting pretty serious with Matthew too. I really like the guy, but it's weird, seeing your mom date."

Sawyer nodded. "Yeah. Anyway, we should probably get back in there. We've got a piece of art to introduce."

But Betzy shook her head. "Actually, I told them we had a canine emergency."

Sawyer's eyes widened. "You did?"

She nodded. "I'll go with you if that's okay."

"I'd like that." He took a step closer and rested a hand at her lower back. It felt good there. Solid and warm. And when she pulled in her next breath, Betzy was reminded, for the hundredth time that evening, of how very good he smelled.

She savored the heavenly scent once they made it to his car, a gorgeous Lamborghini Veneno. He was forced to drive the coupé slowly until they reached the interstate, but there, Sawyer sank the pedal, switched gears, and picked up speed.

Exhilaration shot through her in a tingly rush as the night-lights sped by in a blur. "I *love* this thing," she said.

He glanced over and grinned. "You do?"

"Oh, yeah. I almost bought one myself."

"What did you get instead?" he asked.

She could barely hold back the grin as she replied. "A Bugatti Chiron, black."

"With the metallic blue accents?"

She nodded.

He blew out a whistle. "That's my girl."

She liked hearing him say that.

A bit of tension seemed to drain from his shoulders. Perhaps conversation was a good distraction. He probably needed it.

The truth was, worries over missing the live appearance were starting to eke into her mind, but Betzy pushed them aside to focus on him.

It wasn't exactly the hardest task. Sawyer Kingsley might deal largely with real estate on the east coast, but he owned the larger portion of her LA heart.

"Didn't you used to have a Porsche?"

"Still got it," he said. "I switch off between them. Back in the city I have a Lykan Hypersport."

Her eyes widened. "You're kidding. I thought you used a driver back home."

Sawyer's eyes narrowed for a blink as he stared at the road ahead, thoughtful. "*This* is home to me," he said. And as if the words alone hadn't jumpstarted her heart enough, he darted a look at her—fleeting, but pointed. He wanted her to know that his heart *wasn't* in NYC. And heaven help her, she liked hearing that more than he'd ever know.

She gulped as the new flare of heat settled over her skin.

"But you're right," he finally said. "I rarely drive in the city. I can't wait to get the Lykan here and really break her in."

Betzy nodded, but inwardly, she was dissecting his words. This was the first time she'd heard him talk about coming home to stay in years. It was reassuring, and made her all the more hopeful.

What if? What if they really could have the fairytale romance she'd always dreamed of?

A mean wave of doubt rose at the very idea. *Come on, Betzy. Stop being such a dreamer. Haven't you learned by now?*

A vision of Sawyer kissing that woman in the elevator shot to her mind. And then there was her ugly breakup with Marcus Creighton. Sure, she'd developed feelings for the guy, but Betzy couldn't deny that dating him had been more of an attempt to prove she could get over Sawyer after the New Year's blowout.

A shiver ran through her at the ugly thoughts, but she chose to indulge them just the same. They'd keep her from getting her hopes up. Sawyer had agreed to do her a favor. He cared about her, and even more, he felt a level of loyalty toward her family.

Betzy's thoughts carried her all the way to the clinic, and soon Sawyer was opening her car door.

She glanced at the hand he held out before lifting her gaze to meet his. A flare of heat shot through her as he gave her a soft, almost sad-looking grin. She'd give anything to know what was happening in that head of his.

Looking back to his hand, Betzy reached out and placed her palm in his. A rush of tingles pushed through her at his touch.

"Thanks."

She caught a glimpse of Kellianne Kingsley through the glass. Ted, she guessed, sat beside her, rubbing a hand along her back.

Inwardly, Betzy sent a prayer up to the heavens. Sawyer and his mom had become like family to her, and she had a deep love for them both. She'd made the right choice in coming, that much was clear, but that didn't change the situation at hand. Without an adequate public appearance, the upcoming proposal could look like a hoax.

She only hoped that, after missing the most crucial part of tonight's banquet, they'd still be able to pull off the ploy.

CHAPTER 11

Sawyer sank into the couch with a yawn, eyeing old Mario as he sprawled over the length of his doggie bed, his favorite toy at his side—a ratty old stuffed elephant with the trunk torn off.

"I'm so glad he's alright," he said with a sigh.

"Me too," Betzy said, taking a seat on the opposite end of the couch.

Sawyer shifted his gaze from the dog to the empty couch cushion between them. The lamp at her back, bright against the darkness of the room, lit her up like an angel. One who'd taken a seat decidedly far away from him.

"Tsk, tsk." He shook his head. "We're a little more familiar with each other than *this*, aren't we?" He waved a hand toward the gap between them.

Betzy stiffened slightly, holding his gaze like she was waiting for him to say more.

He didn't. Only smiled as he enjoyed her discomfort.

"You want me to scoot over?" she asked, surprise tinting her voice.

Sawyer patted the couch. "Yep. We *are* supposed to get engaged soon..."

A small giggle sounded at her throat. "Why don't *you* scoot over?"

He shot a glance at the dog. "This seat's closer to Mario. And he nearly died of plant poisoning an hour ago." Just saying it aloud brought back the anxiety of those moments in the waiting area. The horrible worry over losing his little buddy who, according to vets, still had a few good years left in him. So long as he stayed out of the bulbs at Ted's place, that is.

"That's true," Betzy said, but she still didn't move in closer.

"Plus," Sawyer added, "I was the first one to sit down, remember? *You* were the one who decided to sit so far away." He liked teasing her. Liked watching the wheels in her head turn as she tipped to one side, a half-grin pulling at her lips.

He patted the seat again. "Come on," he encouraged. "You and I are together, remember? We need to act like it. If you pull this stunt up at the cabin, your grandma's not going to buy our little ploy."

Her expression shifted suddenly. Serious now. "You're right." She stood to her feet and began to pace the room. Back, forth, then back again.

Sawyer had been trying to pull his gaze off Betzy's legs half the night. He hadn't done a great job at it. And now that she was strutting before him, those stiletto heels enhancing the curvy shape of her long legs, the battle started anew.

"How are we going to do this?" Betzy asked. Her quick glance into the darkness out the front window said she was checking to see if Mom and Ted were back yet. The two had gone out for a bite to eat after all the excitement, allowing Sawyer and Betzy to bring Mario home.

"You're totally right. Grandma knows my body language and she knows my personality…"

"Above all that," he said, a concern of his own coming to mind. "She knows *you*. Will she really think you've fallen for the Kingsley boy?" His heart dropped as he asked the bold question. One he might not want the answer to.

Betzy stopped pacing and shot him a look he couldn't read. Brow furrowed, face scrunched slightly. "Are you kidding? Everyone knows I was in love with you. We had a *marriage* contract, for crying out loud. Of *course* they'll believe it. On *my* end at least."

His pulse spiked for a beat, but Sawyer was quick to put it right once more. The marriage contract—they'd written that when they were eight years old. He knew she had a childhood crush on him at the time. One that likely faded before she hit her teens.

"How did your mom take it?" she asked.

Sawyer thought back on the conversation he'd had with her. "She was fine with it." No sense in telling her how leery Mom was that he'd get his heart broken.

Betzy nodded, her face thoughtful as she tucked an auburn lock of hair behind one ear. "You know, in the article, they list my love for fast cars—among other things—as one of my off-kilter, destined-to-be alone symptoms."

She let out a humorless laugh. "Oh, *and* the fact that I like to be behind the wheel. Like the guy should have to drive every time. Somehow, according to freaking *Slipper Magazine* and their statistical calculations of all the rich loners out there, that makes me less *marriage material* and more spinster-bound."

Her cheeks were turning red, the way they did when her temper flared.

"If you ask me," Sawyer said, "I'd say it's just the opposite. The fact that you know your cars, that you appreciate the models and makes and what sets them apart—I think it's sexy." He studied her reaction, then reveled in the reluctant smile pulling at her lips.

"No you don't," she said softly.

Sawyer nodded. "I do too. Now get over here, park your butt on this couch, and let's practice cuddling."

"*Cuddling?* My family knows I'm not a cuddler."

"Well, maybe that excuse worked for your ex-boyfriend, but it doesn't work for me." This time he patted his chest, indicating she should rest her head against him. "This relationship has to look different from the one with what's-his-name if it's going to convince anyone."

Betzy glanced out the window once more before settling her eyes back on him. "And if your mom comes home?"

"All the better," he said. "She'll be proud of us for practicing our part. Like when we used to do our homework together."

Dang, he liked seeing those dimples.

Betzy laughed now, a cute little giggle as she shook her head. "Fine. You're probably right."

"I am."

"And you know what?" she said, stepping around the coffee table. "I was thinking...I know we missed the live stream tonight, but there might be a leak about us being together at the vet. It's possible one of the staff members recognized us."

Sawyer felt his smile falter. "That's true."

"So it might even be better," she continued. "One appearance at the auction, another at the animal hospital with your sick dog. And only a girlfriend would go along for something like that, right? It'll probably make it all the more convincing."

"Yep." Sawyer tried to force the grin back onto his face, but his inner wheels were stuck in the shifty terrain of Betzy's words. She'd been very comforting while he waited for news of Mario's condition. He didn't like thinking that she'd been wrapped up in appearances during such a time.

That wasn't the Betzy he knew. He hoped she hadn't changed over the years. He'd always loved the traits that set her apart from most in her class. Her compassion for others, appreciation for some of the small things, and her overall freedom from the often binding ties of society. He'd fallen in love with her because of those traits. And stayed in love with her after all these years.

But what if he no longer knew the real Betzy Benton?

That question floated through his mind as she made her way to the center of the couch. She glanced at him over her shoulder briefly, seeming to gage the distance, then lowered herself onto the cushion at last. Instead of scooting back and getting comfortable, she stayed perched on the edge, arms still folded across her chest.

"Wow, this is convincing even me," he teased. "I'm feeling all warm and fuzzy right now."

Betzy covered her face and groaned. "I'm not good at this, I told you." He felt her frustration in those words. Enough to remind him of her fragile condition at the country club when she'd told him about the article. It bothered him, poked at that need he felt to step up and help her.

"That's probably why Daisy's picking on you," he said. "She thinks you're an easy target. But you don't want to go to all this trouble only to have people believe it's all for show."

"You're right," she agreed. "But the whole affection thing can't be over the top either. We have to find just the right balance."

"True," he agreed. "And that might take a lot of practice."

Betzy covered a grin. "You're bad."

"Actually, I'm *good*. You'd know that if you gave me a chance." Sawyer patted his chest once more. "C'mon. It's cuddle time."

"Okay," she finally said with a nod. "Let me just take off my shoes."

Sawyer dropped his gaze to where her delicate fingers fiddled with the strap around her ankle. And for a reason he couldn't explain, *that* was sexy too. He cleared his throat and turned to look at the Christmas tree while residual heat flared low in his belly.

This is what you get for hardly dating. But really, one look at the woman by his side and the explanation was clear. Any man in his right mind would forgo dating a bunch of random ladies if he could skip right to the perfect woman of his dreams. And now, he'd get to put a ring on it. Even if it *was* just for show.

At last Betzy straightened up, shifted further into the seat, and then moved in closer. He was amused by her aversion to cozying up to him, but the humor faded away as he felt the warmth of her body against his.

Sawyer held very still, gulping as she turned in to face him.

Gently then, Betzy lay a hand on his chest. His heart tried greeting it with three full beats out of rhythm.

At last, she rested her cheek just beneath his shoulder.

Yes. Sawyer could hardly believe how natural it felt to wrap his arm around her. "There you go," he said under his breath. "This isn't so bad, is it?"

She giggled, and the warmth of her breath grazed Sawyer's jaw. Which meant that her mouth wasn't far from his. She smelled good too. Like some sort of rose. Subtle, sweet, and decidedly Betzy.

The next breath he pulled in was tighter, almost jagged, as his pulse sped up a notch.

"No," she said softly, as if it were an afterthought. "This isn't bad at all."

He turned the slightest bit, pressed a kiss to the top of her head, and smoothed his hand slowly up her back, and then along her shoulder, and down her arm. It was the second time he'd kissed her head that night, but he could hardly stop himself.

"You smell good," she said.

He chuckled low in his throat. "I was thinking the same thing about you."

Her warm body shifted as he held her in his arms, the tightness fading breath by breath.

"It's going to be okay, you know?" he assured.

Betzy lifted her head off his chest. "What was that?"

"Life after the article. It's going to be fine."

She pulled back until he met her gaze. Boy, did he love that face. Fair, flawless complexion, wide, blue eyes. Her smile put dimples in her cheeks every time, but there was no hint of those dimples now.

"Do you think I'm doing the wrong thing? By asking you to do this?"

Sawyer held her gaze. Did he think it was necessary? No. But did he understand her reasons for doing it? Definitely. The tricky part lay in the benefits *he'd* reap as they followed through with the plan.

"No," he finally said. "I don't think it's the wrong thing. I don't blame you for wanting to stick it to Daisy."

The lines along her forehead softened, and the tiniest hint of a smile pulled at her full, pink lips. "Thank you." She tucked herself back into place, a perfect fit.

"I felt like...maybe you thought I'd turned into a monster."

"A monster?" His voice shot up an octave. "Why would I ever think that?"

Her fingers started a slow trail along his shoulder, lighting the fuse to that heat low in his belly.

"Because I'm doing something strictly for revenge," she said. "That's not very nice."

Sawyer grinned. There was that innocence he liked about her. "You're mainly saving face. The fact that you get revenge at the same time is just a bonus."

"I don't know if that's true though. If Daisy wasn't the editor of *Slipper Magazine*, I might have been satisfied with rebutting the article like a normal person. You know, talk shows, interviews, social media posts. But no, I had to go get the guy we both wanted and use him to make her jealous."

"The guy you *both* wanted?" The comment reminded him of what his mom said—*he* was the common denominator.

Betzy swatted his arm. "Oh, stop it. You know we wanted you all through school. Along with every other girl. Daisy was just the one who got you. And she threw it in my face every chance she got."

Sawyer's heart thumped out of rhythm. Ca-*clank, ca-clank.*

All through school? No, he hadn't known that at all. "I didn't date Daisy until high school. I figured you stopped liking me by the time we hit puberty."

Betzy only shook her head. "Nope."

"So…through junior high?"

Cheek still resting against his chest, she shook her head subtly. "Past that."

"Into high school?" His voice went tight again.

"More like *through* high school," she corrected.

A rush of heat pulsed through his chest. He only hoped she couldn't feel the sudden racing of his heart. She'd *liked* him during that time? It didn't seem possible. Had Sawyer known that she actually liked him the way that he was back then, would he have bothered going to New York?

Yes. Liking him was different from marrying him.

"Does that mean…" Sawyer ended the question there to rephrase it. "So when I kissed you at the farewell party—did you still have feelings for me then?"

Betzy lifted her face off his chest once more, eyes wide and worried. "No." It sounded more like a denial than an honest answer.

Still, his once-swelling ego shrunk like a freshly popped balloon. "Yeah, right," he teased just the same.

He was closer to Betzy than he'd been in years, and now, she'd dropped a huge bomb by saying she'd had feelings for him. To top it all off, the feel of her fingers tracing down the front of his chest, as absent as it might be, was pulling his mind in an entirely different direction.

"Well," Betzy said with a shrug, *"you're* the one who kissed *me.* So who was *really* the one with a crush that day?"

Sawyer was very glad she hadn't lay back onto his chest. Bolts of lightning were clashing in hot, flustered succession. Now it was his eyes that had gone wide. He held her gaze, cursing the expression that no doubt gave him away.

Say something!

Only he couldn't. There wasn't anything to say. Denying it would make him look like a liar.

Betzy's smile began to fade, softly, slowly, until she narrowed her eyes at him in question. "Why *did* you kiss me?"

His heart thundered harder as the answers rolled through his mind. *Because I was in love with you. Because—from the time we wrote that silly contract—I wanted to make you mine. And to this day, I want you more than ever.*

Betzy tipped her head to one side, seeming to read the answers in his eyes. Slowly then, her hand moved up the side of his neck, causing heat to flare low in his belly once more. Her touch—it was magic.

At once it felt like they were back in that place and time. Like they'd been given a chance to relive the moment. Sawyer gulped past the tightness in his throat, dared himself to wrap a hand around the warm curve of one hip.

Yes. This was what he'd been waiting for all these years. For a moment like this to happen naturally, all on its own, to show them that they were meant to—

"How's little Mario doing?" The sound of his mother's voice

put a fast stop to the action. And there was no mistaking—there *would* have been action. Had Mom walked through that door thirty seconds later, he and Betzy would have been smack in the middle of a dang good kiss.

Betzy shot off the couch and onto her feet. "Fine. He's fine. We've just been sitting by him."

Sawyer shot her a questioning look. It wasn't like they were back in grade school.

Betzy snatched her shoes off the floor, plopped back onto the opposite side of the couch, and slipped into them.

Now Mom's warning would be even greater. He could really get his heart hurt in this one.

Sawyer forced himself to stand, still reeling from disappointment, and wandered into the kitchen to look for his keys. Mom chatted with Betzy beside the Christmas tree, something about the cabin. There was a fair amount of snow up there, according to Betzy. It wouldn't compare to the Colorado slopes Mom planned to ski with Ted, but the cabin did have a small ski resort nearby.

Sawyer wondered what the week ahead would look like. He looked forward to the mild snow. Even more, he looked forward to spending time with Betzy. Would they get another chance to recreate the moment they'd missed out on just now?

A fresh ache tore through him from the disappointment. They'd been so close. He shook his head, snatched the keys off the counter, and shuffled back into the front room.

Hearing Betzy and Mom in conversation, watching their faces as they related on the topic of wrapping paper of all things, Sawyer couldn't help but crave the future he'd dreamt of all the more.

His mind shot to the task Betzy had circled on her list—the one about convincing her grandma that they were, in fact, in love. He liked the idea. This might prove to be a very nice week after all.

With that thought, Sawyer cleared his throat, dangled the key ring from his finger, and grinned when they turned his way. "Guess I better get Betzy back home."

The article said she liked to hold onto the wheel, huh? He was man enough to let her do that. Of course, where this ruse was concerned, Sawyer had a plan of his own. One that helped Betzy see they were right for one another after all.

Sawyer Kingsley could be more than just her fake fiancé. He could be the man she'd always wanted.

"What do you say?" Sawyer said, shifting his gaze from Mom to Betzy. "Want to take the wheel?"

CHAPTER 12

*B*etzy rested a box of fresh groceries on the countertop and pulled in a breath of crisp, mountain air. She loved being at the cabin no matter the season, but nothing beat coming up here at Christmastime. Especially when the heavens had gifted them with a few fresh inches of powdery white snow.

She glanced toward the large, central staircase to see Sawyer helping Grandma take her things up to her preferred room. Mom and Matthew were getting settled in their rooms on the main floor, directly across from one another.

Betzy grinned. That was another thing she loved about their getaway in the woods. Here, they lived more like the rest of society. Or close to it. Carrying their own bags, driving their own cars, often even cooking their own food. At least their own snacks after the private chef was done for the evening.

Soon, Matthew's daughter, Emmy, would come with her

two kids, Lilly and Link. Betzy couldn't wait. The small children had a way of brightening every event.

"So, you got the most eligible bachelor of NYC to agree to propose to you?" Duke asked Betzy as he stacked a few drinks in the fridge.

Zander, Duke's twin, nudged him with his elbow. "Shut up, man. You're going to make it awkward."

"It's already awkward," Duke hissed. "Pretend that we're going to get married. Who does that?"

Zander snatched one of Duke's favorite drinks and cracked it open. "Shut up, man. Or I'll tell everyone about the stupid thing *you* did."

Betzy rolled her eyes. She knew Duke well enough. He wasn't as rude as he let on. But as she looked at the exchange between her twin brothers in the quiet pause, she realized that something was off. What exactly did Zander have on him?

They stared at each other, those perfectly proportioned faces—identical save Duke's scruff—a reflection of the same, I-dare-you glare.

Duke's eye twitched. And suddenly he was reaching out, snatching the drink from Zander, and tipping it back.

"Ahh," he said after a big gulp of it. He bumped Zander as he headed toward the back deck. "I knew you wouldn't tell."

Zander's nostrils flared. "He signed up for some wedding game show. You have to marry someone you've never even met if you get picked."

Duke stopped walking, the drink, partway to his lips, hovering in the pause.

Zander glared at the back of his head. "Want me to say it louder next time?"

Duke didn't respond.

"That's what I thought." Zander moved his gaze to Betzy and gave her a knowing grin.

Betzy waited until Duke made it onto the patio before speaking up. "Thank you. And is that true?"

Zander shrugged. "He was dealing with the whole Winston thing."

She tipped her head. The whole Winston thing encompassed the overdose of their youngest brother. It seems they all did things that didn't make sense after that.

"Are Camila and James on their way?" Mom asked as she wandered into the kitchen. She headed straight to the chilled wine cabinet and surveyed the selection.

"Yeah," Zander answered. "They'll be here soon."

"Well, I have to say," Grandma Lo said as she made her way toward the kitchen as well, a gorgeous-looking Sawyer in tow. "It sure is nice having Sawyer here at the cabin with us again. You haven't come since you were a kid," she added.

Sawyer nodded. "Yeah, it's been a while." He locked eyes with Betzy across the room, a heated look that made her toes tingle. It was a good thing he hadn't pulled out the smolder card in years past. She might have asked him to propose to her sooner.

Suddenly, a short movement caught her eye. Grandma was looking between the two of them, back and forth, seeming to survey the exchange. She grinned then, and stepped over to the wine cabinet with Mom. "What have we got here?" she asked.

Betzy moved toward Sawyer, meeting him halfway, and noticed him blow out a breath through pursed lips. "You nervous?" she asked in a whisper.

He rolled his shoulders back a few times and grinned. "Not at all." The wink he shot her said that wasn't exactly true. Something about the exchange felt very natural. Even if the two really *were* dating, he'd likely be nervous to spend the week with her entire family.

"Duke said you guys have a few snowmobiles in the garage. Should we go test one out before the rest of the crew gets here?"

It felt as if he'd just asked her out on a date. All the whirls and twirls stirring in her tummy. "Sure. That'd be fun."

"Hey, Betzy, mind helping me with this cork, dear?" Grandma asked. "I'm such a klutz with these things." She motioned for Betzy to follow her onto the back patio, the bottle in one hand, the opener in the other.

Great. She could already feel the scrutiny coming on. Just days ago in Grandma's boutique, Betzy had said she had no idea who she'd marry if she had to choose. On that same day, Sawyer had come up as table conversation while they ogled his bachelor feature. All the while, Betzy had never said she and Sawyer were even interested in each other. And now she'd shown up at the family trip with him by her side.

Sure, Betzy had told Mom to give Grandma a head's up, but she knew that would only raise more questions. Questions she'd have to answer sooner rather than later.

Zander stepped in and put a hand on Sawyer's shoulder. "I'll help him get one of the Ski-doos out of the garage," he said. "Let's go."

Betzy blew out a breath. Thank heavens for Zander. He was good at stuff like this.

A rush of brisk air swept over Betzy's face as she stepped through the patio door behind Grandma Lo.

Bright, glistening snow clung to the tall, naked redwoods and needle covered pines, creating a spectacular winter view.

This part of the deck was covered, but that hadn't stopped a dusting of windswept snow from settling over the wood slats.

The wood-burning pit, complete with an array of log chairs, lay on the lower level of the deck. Grandma opted for the gas-burning fireplace on the upper level, flicked the switch, and motioned Betzy over to the sidebar.

Betzy joined her at the stone-slated bar before taking hold of the bottle and the opener. "How was your ride over?" She centered the corkscrew and began to twist.

"Fine, fine. Matthew drives much too slow for my taste," she griped. "I like it better when you drive."

Betzy grinned. She'd made it through the center of the cork, so she gripped hold of the steel wings and pressed them down nice and slow.

Up, up, and *pop.* Vapor wafted from the bottle top.

Grandma leaned over and gave it a whiff. "Ah, thank you."

Betzy was hoping to slink back into the house for her snow clothes, but she knew she wouldn't get off so easily.

"I thought we could talk a little bit, before we go back in there, about Sawyer." She never was one to beat around the bush.

"Okay," Betzy said, shivering against the cold anew. A tiny bird fluttered in and poked its delicate beak into the thick of a pine tree.

Grandma scooted the bottle aside and rested her elbows on the bar. "You like Sawyer, do you?"

Betzy nodded. "I've always liked him."

"*Liked,* yes. But your mom says you two are dating?"

"Yes. I know I haven't told you, but not that long ago, I started to sense that maybe he had feelings for me, the way I do him." It felt odd saying it aloud, but this was how Betzy wished things would've gone. Long before now.

A bit of sadness threatened to creep in. After their almost-kiss at Kellianne's, Betzy had started to convince herself that perhaps Sawyer's feelings were there after all. But if that were the case, he'd have pursued her a long time ago.

"Anyway," she said, forcing a smile on her face. "We've been kind of exploring that, long distance." She didn't sound too convincing. "Not actual dates, of course, but flirting. Lots of that. And telling each other that…"

"That you like one another?" Grandma finished for her.

"Yes. Exactly."

Betzy knew Grandma well enough to know what her reaction *would* be like if she actually believed her. Her eyes would go wide and teary, and she'd snatch a hard hold of Betzy's shoulders like she did over the dress. Then she'd rave about how exciting it all was and ask for more details.

None of that was happening. Instead, she was getting the woman's skeptical stare. Chin lifted, a quiet peer down the bridge of her nose.

Quick, Betzy, be more convincing.

"I've been in love with Sawyer since I was eight years old." She could hardly believe the words had poured out of her mouth so freely. "Ask the boys. They've probably known it all along. I've always had a crush on him. I guess I've been waiting for him to come home and say he felt the same way."

"Which he has?" she challenged.

No, an inner voice blurted. "Mm hmm." She gulped as a fresh ache tugged at that corner of her heart. The one she'd tried very hard to keep buried. "It's getting pretty serious, actually. That's why he's here."

In the distance, she heard the roar of an engine—Sawyer must be ready with the snowmobile.

"Where in tarnation did the wine go?" Betzy's mom hollered as she shuffled onto the covered deck in a pair of thick padded Christmas socks.

Grandma handed over the bottle. "Pour one for me too, will you, dear?"

"Yep." Mom, surely aware of the topic, scurried back inside. Earlier, while they spoke about the importance of this trip, Mom warned Betzy that if everything went awry, she planned to play ignorant to the ploy. *Most women don't get along so well with their mothers-in-law like I do,* she'd said. *I don't want to risk messing that up.*

Plus, there was Matthew to consider. He and his family hadn't been clued in on the plan either. As Betzy predicted, Mom was certain he'd try to talk them out of it and find a 'higher road.'

"Listen," Grandma said, reaching out to hold Betzy by the arm. This wasn't the excited double arm grab. This was the gentle, one-arm hold. The one reserved for lectures.

"I'm not trying to grill you or anything, Hon, but I want to make sure that if you're with somebody, you're with them for the right reasons. I'd hate for you to get serious with someone just to prove a point."

Prove a point? Whoa.

"Prove *what* point?" she repeated. "To *who?*"

But Grandma only smiled. "To yourself, of course. If someone were to write that type of article about me, the first thing I'd set out to prove is that I could, in fact, get married whenever I darn well pleased."

Betzy grinned. They were a lot alike, in truth. Always had been. Too bad Betzy couldn't admit that right then. She fought back a shiver and shuffled closer the warmth of the nearby gas flames. "Yeah, well, that's not what's happening here."

"Good."

But she could see it in her face. See that she didn't really believe her. And though it wasn't the smartest thing, and though she'd seen how many times it led to disaster, Betzy began to ramble.

"You remember that time I flew all the way out to New York? I said I was going out there to see a friend of mine but then I came back early?"

"You mean over New Years?" she asked.

"Yes. I wasn't going to just see *any* friend. I was going to see him. Because I was in love with him and I thought he loved me too, but then I saw him kissing some chick in the elevator and I freaked out and came home."

"Who was he kissing?" Grandma asked.

"You're missing the point," Betzy said, mainly because she didn't have a clue who he'd been kissing that night. "All I'm saying is that I've loved him forever and now he finally likes me back, and in fact he says he liked me all along and he was just waiting until it was time to move back." *Shut up, Betzy. You're making it worse.*

Grandma gave her arm a pat. "If you two like each other, I'm

110

happy for you. But don't go around acting foolish all because some article is toying with your head. Those people don't know you. They can't predict the future better than anyone else, so they can *shove* it."

"Cheers to that," Mom hollered from inside. "Now come get your drink, Lorraine."

"I'm coming, Claudia," she assured before turning back to Betzy. "As for you, I just don't want to see you get hurt, okay? Sometimes men, they...they act like they want *one* thing, but really—"

"He's not like that," Betzy blurted. She wasn't about to stand there and listen to the *men can be jerks* talk like she was some naïve teenager.

"I'm sure he's a sweet guy. Just...be careful. I don't want to see you get hurt."

An ugly recollection shot to mind. The way Marcus had used her so blatantly. And now, he'd given *Slipper Magazine* an earful since, apparently, he hadn't done enough damage. Grandma had good reason to question her judgment after that mess.

"Thanks, Grandma," Betzy finally said. She wrapped an arm around her and gave her a squeeze. "Now go in there and get your glass."

She did, leaving Betzy alone with her thoughts. Grandma didn't know all the facts, but still, her warning caused a pool of doubts to rise up in Betzy's gut. Could she really let herself fall even deeper for Sawyer, only to send him on his way once the holidays were through?

What Grandma didn't know is that Sawyer *was* playing a

part. A part Betzy had asked him to play, of course, but that didn't mean lines wouldn't get blurred.

They were sure to. For Sawyer, it'd be all for show. For Betzy, it'd be different.

She'd buried that part of her heart to forget about Sawyer, but now she'd watered the seed and allowed it to sprout. As Betzy spent the week with him, a full-on tree would grow, complete with deep roots, reaching limbs, and fruit she'd be so tempted to taste.

But where would she end up in the wake of it all?

Be careful, Grandma had warned. Betzy nodded, musing that she would, in fact, heed to her counsel after all. Perhaps there was a way to do this while still guarding her heart.

CHAPTER 13

*S*awyer closed his laptop and tucked it into his bag.
Thank heavens he'd been able to get online and take
care of a few things. Several deals were set to close over the
next few days, and as much as he encouraged clients to send
questions to the office, many insisted on going directly through
him via email or text.

As if on cue, his phone let out a chime once his laptop was
put away. Good thing it was only seven a.m. here on the west
coast. If all went well, he'd be able to wrap up his work before
Betzy was awake. A grin crossed his lips as he recalled their
time spent on the snowmobile. James and Camila had joined
them once they arrived, along with Zander and Duke.

The time chasing over the snowy ground with her siblings
gave Sawyer a taste of the life he'd always dreamed of having.
Dinnertime was even better. A large family gathered around a
big table, laughter echoing clear up to the log rafters.

Their extra visitors, Matthew's daughter and grandkids, had

shown up. Lilly was five and her older brother Link was seven. Dang, they were cute. The kids' father, who was serving overseas, hadn't been able to join them. Sawyer couldn't imagine. Even as he considered it once more, he felt a swell of gratitude for those who sacrificed and served in such a way.

His phone buzzed once more, breaking into his musings. He snatched it off the side table and glanced at the screen.

Ryan: *Are you finally going to go after Betzy Benton this year? If so, I want details.*

Sawyer chuckled under his breath and tapped out a reply. *Maybe I am. I'm actually at her family cabin as we speak.*

May as well warm Ryan up to what would come. His phone buzzed back a second after he hit send.

Ryan: *That's what I'm talking about, you lucky dog. Same room?*

Sawyer rolled his eyes as he replied: *Separate rooms. One thing at a time, my friend.*

Ryan: *Yeah, yeah. Sounds thrilling. 2 grand says you don't even get past 2nd base.*

"Jerk," Sawyer said through a laugh. Ryan had his mind made up that Betzy would be a prude. Not that it was any of his business.

Sawyer stared at the text for a blink, wondering if he should clue his uncle in on the whole scheme. *No.* That'd be a bad idea. The guy was trustworthy enough, but he tended to toe the line when keeping secrets.

But he should probably hint to how close he and Betzy were getting since Sawyer would propose to her before Christmas. A grin pulled at his lips as an idea came to mind.

Sawyer: *10 grand says she agrees to marry me by Christmas.*

He hesitated to hit send, but only for a moment. Heck, Ryan

knew Sawyer had a one-track brain with Betzy's name on it. It shouldn't come as much of a surprise.

Ryan: *Sounds like she's more of a prude than I thought if you have to put a ring on it first.*

Sawyer shook his head and tapped out a reply. *You're a jerk, you know that?* Only this time he didn't hit send. Instead, he set the phone down, sank into the lounge chair beneath the lamplight, and pondered his uncle's aversion to the traditional life of love and marriage.

Sawyer didn't relate. From a young age, he'd gotten a rare glimpse into a family that—despite having all the money they could ever need—loved and depended on each other.

The Bentons were generous and kind. They laughed together, played together, and yesterday, Sawyer got to be a part of it in an entirely new way. Of course, he wanted to be with Betzy above all else—her closeness, her touch, her kiss...

Heat stirred low in his belly at the mere thought. Betzy was worried about convincing her grandma their relationship was real. Sawyer knew his feelings were real; there'd be no problem there. But would Betzy be able to let her guard down and get close to him, or did her purpose start and end with getting revenge?

Yesterday hadn't been too much of a challenge, with the activities of the day. Today could be a different story. He'd seen the agenda. It entailed a movie in the cabin's theater and a candy cane making lesson, courtesy of James' wife, Camila. Boy, were Lilly and Link excited about that. Then they'd finish off the day by decorating the tree.

Sawyer wandered out to the kitchen, surprised to be greeted with the tempting aroma of a rich, morning brew. He strode over to the coffee maker, glad to see there was a full pot, and reached for a mug.

"Good morning," Betzy's voice came from behind.

Sawyer glanced over his shoulder, scanned over the empty couches and lounge chairs, and furrowed his brow. "Where are you?"

A soft little giggle sounded next. "On the floor by the fireplace."

Sawyer took a few steps to see past the corner lounge chair and caught sight of a pair of feet propped up on the mantel. The gas fireplace was on, he realized.

"Oh, hi there." He abandoned his mug and stepped into the room. "How'd you sleep?"

"I slept alright." She grinned at him as he approached, that gorgeous smile causing those dimples to shine.

Betzy looked beautiful, of course. A short, pajama-style pair of shorts with an oversized sweatshirt. It reminded him of the way she looked back in high school after playing soccer. Cheeks flushed, hair pulled back in a ponytail, and that flirtatious grin making his heart melt.

His gaze traveled down the length of her slender legs, all the way to her bare feet, complete with red polish. Already the distant sound of Christmas music played softly from the speakers.

Sawyer almost took a seat on the nearby chair, until he remembered himself. He'd given Betzy crap for not sitting next to him on the couch, hadn't he? Besides, more than anyone, he hoped to convince *Betzy* that the two had something real. Even if she hadn't realized it over the years.

He took a seat on the mantel beside her feet, then stretched his legs out alongside hers.

She looked up at him for a blink, her expression caught between surprise and intrigue. "How did *you* sleep?" she asked. "Was the bed comfortable?"

He nodded. "Yes, very. Thank you." Several times over the years, Sawyer had seen Mr. Benton rubbing Claudia's feet while they lounged together in the front room. Sawyer considered doing the same.

Before he could talk himself out of it, he wrapped a hand around Betzy's slender ankle and cupped her heel.

"Foot rub?" he asked.

Betzy hedged, but Sawyer pressed a thumb into the side of her heel—once, and then twice.

"That feels nice," she admitted.

Satisfaction shot through him as he took hold of her foot with both hands now, working his way up the center. "You know, that rug is probably thick enough that you can make something similar to snow angels."

"Rug angels?" she said with a giggle. At once she extended her arms out to either side and flapped them up and down, matting the rug with her movement.

"Hey, it actually works," he said.

Those dimples sank into her cheeks once more. "All I need is my halo."

Sawyer gulped. "I'm pretty sure you were born with one."

He hadn't meant to say it aloud, but the truth was, Betzy had always been like a living angel to him.

"Yeah, right," she said with a laugh.

"No, it's true. If I play along, I'll have to be a snow devil to match the horns I've earned over the years. I am *no* angel."

Betzy held his gaze, a wistful look in her eyes. "Well, then you've had me fooled."

He cleared his throat, dropped his gaze back to the massage, where he pressed circles along the balls of her foot. "I really like being here with you," he admitted. When she didn't reply right away he added to it. "And your whole family too. You've got a pretty incredible group."

Betzy sighed. "I think so too. I'm really glad Matthew's daughter brought the kids up. They're adorable, aren't they?"

"Oh, yeah. I always knew I'd have kids of my own, but I pictured being an uncle too. You know, where I get to goof off with the kid, show him a good time, then send him home with their mom or dad. Kind of like my Uncle Ryan was with me."

"I'd love to be an aunt," Betzy said. "With those guys, it feels like I already am in a way. I wonder how long Camila and James will wait to have kids."

"It's lucky that you have such a large family," Sawyer said. "I always wanted that." He switched feet and repeated the motion on her other foot. It grew quiet, save Betzy's occasional whine of approval as Sawyer moved from the bottom to the top of her foot.

"You're very good at this," she praised. "Want me to do yours next?"

Sawyer shook his head.

"Then maybe you can join me down here," she suggested, giving the rug a pat.

What was this? She was trying to step out of her comfort zone, was she?

"Okay," he agreed. Sawyer moved from the mantel to his knees and made his way to her side. He grunted as he lay flat on the plush rug beside her. "Let's spoon," he said, matching the bend in her knees, the curve of her back. A stack of decorative pillows lay nearby. He snatched a thin looking one, propped it beneath his head and hers, and wrapped an arm around her waist.

She felt more delicate than he'd imagined, and oh, so warm. The heat from the fireplace had warmed his back well, but the sensation that ran through Sawyer at the feel of Betzy in his arms was in a class of its own.

That sweet but subtle scent of her toyed with him as he pulled in a breath. May as well drink it in.

With that thought, Sawyer tucked his face into the nook of her neck and sighed. "This feels good," he said. And it did. Having her close, wrapped snug in his arms, he couldn't imagine anything better. Here, she was safe. Protected. Loved.

An ache tore through him at the near desperation he felt to play that role. To be that man in her life.

Betzy wiggled slightly beneath his touch. "Your breath tickles," she said softly.

Sawyer lifted a brow. Then moved in so that his lips were grazing her warm, silky skin. "It does, does it?" he crooned in a low voice.

"Yes, mmm." The seductive sound, caught between a sigh and whimper, put fire in his belly once more. "Say something else," she urged.

The energy shifted from playful to passionate in a hot blink. How many times had he imagined pressing kisses to her throat? Moving his way up to those pouty lips?

Ever so softly, Sawyer barely grazed the silky slope of her neck with his lips. "Like this?" he asked, hoping she felt even a fraction of the sensations rushing through him.

Betzy didn't answer with words this time. Instead, she reached up, fisted the auburn hair draped over her shoulder, and moved it behind her back; an action that exposed the full, delicate curve of her neck.

Sawyer wasted no time moving in once more. With his lips slightly parted, just a millimeter from her skin, he trailed a slow path up toward her earlobe, his heated breath teasing along the way.

"Betzy," he said, voice low and raspy, his mouth barely grazing her skin.

The action seemed to spark something in her, because suddenly she shrugged onto her back and moved until they were face to face.

Warm, colorful firelight lit her expression as she looked at him, breath jagged, before dropping her gaze to his mouth.

With the urgency of ten years pushing him on, Sawyer closed the gap between them and pressed his lips to hers in a long, fervent kiss.

So good.

He took the next one slower, lingering as he savored each sensation.

The blessed heat of her breath.

The silky pull of her lips.

The tempting taste of her mouth.

A sense of triumph rushed through him—after all this time, he was finally kissing Betzy Benton.

He tipped his head, desperate for more, when a distinct clank sounded from the kitchen.

Betzy was the first to respond. At once, she pushed away from him and sprung up like a jack-in-the-box. "Who's in here?" she called. If *guilty* had a tone of its own, Betzy had found it.

"Me," one of her brothers mumbled. The clank came again. "I need coffee."

Betzy shot from the floor to the mantle, where Sawyer had been sitting moments ago.

Duke, it turned out, shuffled into the living area in a zombie-like state. Until he caught sight of Sawyer on the floor. At once he froze in place, gaze ping-ponging between Betzy, him, then back to Betzy once more.

"What were you two doing in here?"

Sawyer shot a look at Betzy as she blurted a response.

"Nothing. Just talking."

Duke performed a slow, insinuative nod. "Uh huh. Yeah, right."

"No, really," Betzy persisted. Only Sawyer couldn't understand why. Why would she try to hide the fact that they'd been kissing? Was she ashamed of him after all? Worried about what her family might think if she did, in fact, have feelings for him?

He considered making some sort of joke to ease the tension, but he was too bothered by the situation to even try. Instead, Sawyer hoisted himself off the ground, put the throw pillow back in place, and made his way to the patio.

"Busted..." He heard Duke say as he closed the door behind him.

Who knew how Betzy would respond to that. All Sawyer

knew was that he hadn't anticipated this type of reaction. He didn't want to be someone she was ashamed of.

Beyond that, he hadn't expected things to move as quickly as they had. One minute he'd been rubbing her feet, the next they were well on their way to a make-out session.

Residual heat pulsed through him at the recollection of that kiss. And call him crazy, but he was pretty sure she'd been the one to start it by turning to face him. Sure, he'd teased her a little first, but she'd encouraged him by moving her hair out of the way.

Sawyer shook his head, unable to make sense of it. Apparently, he was good enough for the *public* to think they might marry, since it would help her save face in a pinch. But heaven forbid her *family* actually think it was real. Heck, if she wasn't so worried that her grandma would expose the ruse for what it was, Betzy probably wouldn't have invited him to the cabin at all.

Sawyer suddenly felt like nothing more than a stage prop in Betzy's little show. Men like Marcus Creighton, as slimy and selfish as he was, landed among the elite with their name and family alone. Forget the fact that he squandered his daddy's money and bankrupted the business.

Somehow it was Sawyer who'd never measure up. Money or no, he was still Sawyer Kingsley.

Good enough for stepping up in a pinch.

Good enough to play the temporary lover.

But not good enough for her.

That cruel, inner voice of Sawyer's was kicking up once again.

Only this time, he had to admit that it wasn't as convincing as it'd been before. Perhaps Betzy really did have feelings for him. Feelings she wouldn't allow herself to give in to.

Their time in front of the fireplace said it all, didn't it?

Yes. And as he mused back on the way her lips met his, the passion and need he'd felt in that kiss, one thing was very clear: there'd been nothing fake about it.

CHAPTER 14

*B*etzy smiled up at the camera as Grandma counted down for a picture. Inwardly, she was reliving a play-by-play of the incredible kiss she and Sawyer shared earlier that day.

"One."

The feel of Sawyer's lips on her skin.

"Two."

Betzy, turning to face him.

"Three."

Sawyer moving in, pressing his masterful lips to hers, and giving her a kiss that outshone the unforgettable kiss they shared over ten years ago.

She blinked after the camera flashed, and forced herself to come back to the present. The kitchen, bright compared to the dark evening outside, had transformed into a candy factory fit for the North Pole. Now was the time for making candy canes. Or, candy shapes, since the pliable vines could be shaped into whatever the mind could imagine. Until the candy solidified, that is.

Camila and James were heading the project. The couple demonstrated a whole lot of team work while one kneaded the massive ball of mint flavored candy while the other smoothed pieces at a time into one long vine, only to cut and distribute them to the waiting crowd.

When she wasn't distracted by thoughts of Sawyer's kiss, Betzy was admiring the way the newlywed couple complimented one another so well. James really was the perfect one to get married first. She hoped the example would help Zander relax about the idea of getting serious with someone, and that Duke might shed his undying need to be, as he put it, shackle-free.

She glanced over at Sawyer, who was sandwiched between Lilly and Link. They'd taken a real liking to him, and Zander too.

"Hold up your candy this time," Grandma prompted. Betzy glanced at the selection among them. Mom and Matthew had shaped their latest candy strips into wreaths. Duke had simply wrapped his around his finger, while Betzy had opted for a traditional cane.

She couldn't help but grin as Lilly proudly lifted the golf putter and ball for the camera. Something Sawyer had helped her with.

Zander and Link held up what looked like footballs, wide grins aimed right at the camera while the flash went off once more.

At the other side of the counter, James reached for the scissors. "Who's ready for more?" he asked.

"I am," cheered the kids as they jumped up and down.

"Will you help me do a race car this time?" Lilly asked Sawyer through a set of dark lashes.

"I'll sure try," he said.

"And will you help me do a basketball this time?" Link asked Zander.

Dang, they were cute. Emmy had snuck off to take what Betzy assumed was a much-needed nap. She could only imagine how much they all missed having *Dad* around.

Betzy was glad the men could step in and take part in the activity with them, but she'd be lying if she said she wasn't looking forward to getting Sawyer alone once more.

The thing was, that kiss had led Betzy to one very important conclusion: she was bound to get hurt no matter how this thing went. She'd been in love with him for all these years. And now, she had the chance to be close to him, spend family time with him like she'd always dreamed of, and if she was lucky, she'd even get to steal a few more kisses along the way.

Maybe he was, like Grandma warned, just being a guy— willing to take what he could get from her. But maybe, just maybe he secretly felt the same. But would Betzy ever find out if she was set on keeping him at arms' length?

No. So it was decided. She'd let that seed in her heart grow into a massive, thriving tree—Sawyer's tree—and she'd worry about how to prune it when the time came.

Betzy stared at her candy vine as she shaped the top part into a shepherd's hook. Already it was starting to harden. Just like her resolve. Firm and unmovable—that was her.

"Why doesn't anyone ask *me* to make something?" Duke asked over her shoulder. He tugged the hardened spiral candy off his finger, inspected it for a blink, then clanked it against the counter where it broke into pieces.

"Cuz you'll break ours," Link accused.

Duke rolled his eyes. "Kids hate me."

"Oh, I bet I know who you're doing *that* for," Betzy heard Lilly say next.

"Shh," Sawyer said. "We don't want her to see it yet. We need two more. Get two more."

"Go ahead and make your next ones," Grandma instructed, "then I'm going to get another picture."

Betzy nudged Duke with her arm and whispered conspiratorially. "What shape should we do this time?"

Duke shrugged. "How about question marks since no one knows what's real or fake around here?"

James flung the warm ropes of candy one by one. "Duke, Betzy, Zander," he mumbled as he went.

Betzy toyed with the warm candy while glancing at the kids clustered up to the guys.

"Okay," Lilly hissed. "It's ready. Go give it to her."

"Yeah," Link cheered. "Do it."

Betzy watched as Sawyer's face warmed beneath the groups' collective gaze. He was prying something off the counter top. Then, with the fairly large piece of artwork in both hands, he stepped around the kids and made his way to her.

"For you, Betzy Boo," he said with a wink. It was a nickname he'd given her back in grade school; she'd nearly forgotten all about it.

The trio had shaped candy sticks into a large heart with an arrow through it.

"Is that because you love her?" Lilly asked through a toothy grin.

The clatter died down. The mumbling and laughing too. Betzy could have sworn the stereo system tapped down a notch in the quiet beat as well.

"What was that?" Grandma Lo asked from behind the lens.

"I asked if he picked a heart because he loves Betzy," Lilly hollered.

Betzy's heart thumped out of rhythm.

All eyes shot to Sawyer as they awaited his response. Betzy couldn't imagine what he might say back to that.

Sawyer glanced from one person to the next before he turned to look at her. His eyes narrowed as he held her gaze, and a rush of heat swelled deep in her chest.

"Yes," he said at last.

A ripple of goosebumps rushed up her arms.

"Let's get everyone to say cheese," Grandma blurted.

Betzy slipped a wobbly hand beneath one half of the candy-shaped heart and moved in closer to Sawyer, heart pounding in double rhythm. Sure, he'd said it to please Lilly and the crowd. But he'd said it just the same.

"Uh, oh," James said through a smile. "Isn't that mistletoe up there?"

"Looks like you two have to kiss," Camila added.

Betzy scanned nearly the entire kitchen before looking over her other shoulder where Duke stood, dangling a sprig of mistletoe over her head.

"Yay!" Lilly cheered while jumping up and down. "Now you get to kiss her."

Link's reaction was a little different. The kid groaned and slapped a hand to his forehead. "Oh no, just get it over with."

"Will you make sure Zander doesn't try and steal the heart we made?" Sawyer asked Lilly while motioning to the piece on the countertop.

Anticipation rushed through Betzy in a warm, tingly wave. Heaven help her. Just what kind of new age therapy would she need to get Sawyer out of her head after this?

Sawyer searched her face for a moment more before locking his eyes on hers. And suddenly, a wide, triumphant-looking grin spread over his face, one that read *brace yourself.*

He started by placing a solid hand at the center of Betzy's back. Then, without further warning, he dipped her back, using his leg for support until he hovered over her. It all happened so quickly she nearly lost her breath.

Whistles and cheers broke out over the kitchen.

Sawyer lowered himself then, her heart hammering harder with every inch he neared, until their lips barely touched.

"Hi," he said. And then he kissed her. She assumed he'd make it short and sweet, considering their audience, but he didn't. Instead he kissed her long, slow, and alluring.

Sawyer was good at this. Too good. She would accuse him of cheating, but she wasn't sure *what* he was cheating at. The game of convincing half of their company that they were in love, or the potential game he was playing with her heart?

The group was still cheering.

Betzy hadn't planned to get lured into a moment of passion, but the man was magic and he'd somehow turned her into a pool of swooning delight.

Suddenly Sawyer grinned against her lips, sprung her right back into place, and tapped a tiny kiss to the tip of her nose.

When Betzy wobbled back, Sawyer steadied her by cupping her elbow.

"You're welcome," Duke mumbled from behind.

Once the chatter died down, Betzy reached for another candy vine and began twisting it into a heart of her own. It was in that moment she became aware of Grandma's scrutinizing gaze.

She hoped the stubborn woman wasn't onto them. Grandma could be persistent, and the last thing Betzy needed was for someone in her own family to sabotage her plan.

It took her a moment to remember the reason for that plan, but soon enough she did—revenge. Yes, for what Daisy had done. That's why she was doing this.

But then she recalled Lily's question—*Is that because you love her?* Betzy pictured the look in Sawyer's eye when he answered that question with a fervent *yes.*

It was moments like that that made Betzy wonder if what Grandma implied was true. What if Betzy really was trying to prove something more to herself than anyone else?

She'd written Sawyer off not long ago, swearing she'd never let herself hope for him again. But what if this was her way of opening up to Sawyer one last time?

Just then Duke leaned in once more. "Lucky Sawyer," he said under his breath. "All the benefits of being the fiancé without the commitment."

Betzy shot him a look over her shoulder.

"Fake fiancé—with *benefits*," Duke mumbled and grinned.

She was tempted to hush her older brother, but with as loud as the group was, Betzy knew there wasn't a need. Perhaps what she really wanted to do is silence the words in her own mind. Duke's comment touched on Grandma's warning about men and their intentions, something she hadn't felt applied to Sawyer.

It didn't, she assured herself. Sawyer and Duke's personalities were miles apart.

Still, that very concern lingered at the forefront of Betzy's mind as they finished up in the kitchen. Enough that she was second-guessing their kiss that morning, something she didn't want to do.

Betzy forced herself to focus on a bit of inner talk. Sawyer wasn't like most men. He wouldn't use her that way. Heck, the guy could have any woman he wanted.

By the time they moved on to decorating the tree, she'd managed to push Duke and Grandma's comments out of her head.

"This is a cute picture of you," Sawyer said as he lifted a framed ornament for her to see. "I remember this one. What is it, eighth grade?"

Betzy leaned in to scrutinize the photo in the center of the wreath-shaped ornament. Red hair tucked into a high ponytail, way too much blush, and a wide grin on her face. "Yes," she said. "Eighth grade. I was *really* into rouge that year."

Sawyer only grinned, eyeing the picture once more before lifting it to a branch. "I was really into *you* that year," he admitted.

Betzy felt herself blush at his words. It probably looked like she'd slipped back into time where she'd covered her cheeks in pink, but she didn't mind. Hearing Sawyer say things like that was like candy to her soul.

"Hey, Betzy," her mom hollered. "Have you got an extra pair of slippers? My feet are freezing."

"Sure," Betzy said. "I'll grab them. Be right back," she mumbled to Sawyer before heading away from the group.

The sounds of laughter and chatter faded as Betzy made her way back through the kitchen and toward her room. A Christmas melody floated from the speakers, the familiar tune bringing a smile to her lips. She was enjoying herself. Enjoying the time with Sawyer and her family. Even if it wasn't the real thing, playing the role with her lifelong crush was better than she'd imagined it could be.

The thought was interrupted as she passed Sawyer's room and heard a chime from his phone, one indicating he'd just received a text.

She ignored it at first, but as she rounded the corner to go into her room, a thought came to mind. What if Kellianne needed him for something? He'd probably kept it on in case of an emergency. It wouldn't hurt to at least check.

With that, she snatched the extra slippers from her dresser and hurried into Sawyer's room. There, glowing face up on the side table, the device let out another chime.

Quickly, Betzy hovered over the screen to read the text that had popped up.

Ryan: *I'll take your silence as confirmation. Hopefully you can at least work up to holding hands before then.*

Holding hands?

She knew that it was a very bad idea to tap on his phone and read the texts leading up to it, but her curiosity had been piqued.

As quickly as the thought came to her, Betzy swiped the screen, hoping it wouldn't require a password.

It didn't. With that one touch, Betzy had opened the text interactions between Sawyer and his uncle. She set her eyes on the first one she could see at the top of the screen and read from there.

Ryan: *That's what I'm talking about, you lucky dog. Same room?*

Sawyer: *Separate rooms. One thing at a time, my friend.*

Ryan: *Yeah, yeah. Sounds thrilling. 2 grand says you don't even get past 2nd base.*

Sawyer: *10 grand says she agrees to marry me by Christmas.*

Ryan: *Sounds like she's more of a prude than I thought if you have to put a ring on it first.*

Betzy brought a hand to her mouth. A mean ache settled over her as she read over it once more. *One thing at a time, my friend.* That's what Sawyer had said.

It was obvious that his uncle didn't know about the plan. Perhaps this was Sawyer's way of warming him up to the idea. But why hadn't Sawyer defended her after Ryan's ugly comment?

She glared at the phone. "At least work up to holding hands?" Sure, Marcus was right about what he'd said in the article. Betzy hadn't wanted to go that far with him. In fact, she didn't want to go that far with *anyone* who didn't truly love her, and she didn't plan on changing that now.

Was that really all men worried about—how far they were going to get?

First the warning from Grandma, then the comment from

Duke, and now this? Perhaps Sawyer was more like the rest of them than she thought.

Fine. She'd consider herself warned.

If she were smart, Betzy would invalidate every ounce of affection she got from Sawyer. Chalk it all up to men taking what they could get. Then, she'd shift her focus back to her plan instead.

And though Betzy hated the idea, she could already feel herself doing that very thing. It was time to put her focus back on the plan.

CHAPTER 15

*S*awyer tossed and turned in his bed, thoughts of Betzy and that morning kiss heavy on his mind. He was tempted to knock on her door, wake her in the night, and see if she wanted to join him in front of the fireplace once more. Maybe he'd grab a few logs from out back and strike up a wood fire in the double hearth, recreate the moment beside a real crackling fire.

It started out as a playful musing at first, but just as he began to fully entertain the idea, a knock came to his own door. Soft, almost indecipherable.

"Sawyer?" Betzy whispered from the doorway. "Are you awake?"

"Depends on who's asking," he said. "Is this the girl who wants to lay in front of the fireplace with me and kiss?"

She giggled, and he could tell by the gentle sound of footsteps that she'd entered the room. "It's the girl who wants to talk about what you're going to say, at the proposal."

Oh. If he were honest, Sawyer didn't like to be reminded of how, well, fake all of this was.

"Doesn't the guy usually come up with that?" The last thing he wanted to do was recite some spoon-fed lines while the camera rolled.

"Mind if I sit?" He could tell, by the sound of her voice, that she was approaching the foot of his bed.

Sawyer was quick to move his legs. "No, go ahead," he said, giving it a blind pat in the darkness.

"Thanks. I think, considering the circumstance, that it might be better to have it scripted. Just to avoid..."

"Avoid what? Me messing it all up?" A bout of irritation stirred in the pit of his stomach. This was the very thing that kept popping up during their time together. One moment he was confident Betzy was on the same page, feeling the same things, and the next, she'd bring up the plan like it was the only thing on her mind.

"Trust me," he said under his breath. "I know all the right things to say."

She stayed quiet, seeming to look for some benign approach to getting her way. There wasn't one.

Of all the things he'd been asked to do in life, this task was meant for him, and him alone.

"Betzy Benton," he said softly. Sawyer reached for her hand, found it resting over her knee, and sandwiched it between his own. A rush of emotion pushed its way to the surface, fusing his words with all the tenderness he'd use if the moment were real.

"I have loved you since we were eight years old, when I

taught you how to wink. To this day, that wink of yours makes my heart skip at least two full beats."

He paused there, the raw truth in his words causing his throat to tighten.

"I wanted my time in New York to be like that wink, fast and fleeting, so that I could come back to you and make you mine."

She sniffed, and suddenly her hand was trembling.

Sawyer cradled her wrist gently, and dared himself to say more. But Betzy beat him to the punch.

"That's perfect," she said with another sniff. Already she was climbing off the bed. "I changed my mind. I guess you *do* know what to say." With that, Betzy hurried out of the room, closing his door behind her.

Her door closed a moment later.

Sawyer exhaled a breath, heavy with the unspoken words in his heart. He didn't want to lie back down and swallow his thoughts back into the depths they'd lived in for all these years. Instead, Sawyer wanted to burst into Betzy's room, drop onto one knee, and confess it all right then and there.

Adrenaline coursed through him at the mere idea, hot and restless, pushing at him from every inward angle.

I'm not mad about the contract, sweetie. I think it's cute. And we love Sawyer too, trust me. But you're a Benton...

And there it was, his mighty, title-holding friend—fear. Ready to stop him once again from going after the woman of his dreams. Ready to pull him back to reality and remind him that, while he'd accomplished a lot, it still wasn't enough.

Sawyer had been certain, while pouring his heart out to Betzy just then, that she felt the same. He wasn't so sure of that anymore. In fact, it was possible she'd known how very real it was for him, and that she'd wanted to avoid the awkward moment of turning him down and bringing him back to reality. *This is just for pretend, remember? You know that, right?*

Yes. He knew. But Sawyer also knew that Betzy felt something for him. She was simply afraid to admit it. Of course, if she felt the two couldn't really have a future together, what would be the point?

But he wasn't ready to give up just yet. Sawyer had accomplished a lot over the years, and he wanted to still believe that he had a chance at scoring the thing he wanted most—a life with Betzy by his side.

Betzy lay in the center of her bed, a blanket draped over her head to stifle the tears. Sawyer was so sweet to try and flatter her like he had, to give her a taste of what a meaningful proposal would look like. But she knew, as kind and beautiful as his words were, she'd never hear them in the way she hoped. That text with his uncle said it all; this was no more than a game to him.

And the more Betzy considered it, the more she realized that everything in that article was true, all the way down to her fanatical need to be in control. She'd wanted to have control over the proposal as well. She'd written it up, thought she'd nailed it, only to discover that it was vanilla bland compared to Sawyer's.

A deep, aching sigh passed through her lips. She just had to get through this. Then she could move on. But her plan didn't seem as easy as it had days ago.

When it was all said and done, Grandma Lo would be furious, Sawyer would be gone, and Betzy would be left with nothing but her revenge.

Suddenly, that revenge seemed like a hollow prize.

CHAPTER 16

Sawyer kept his eyes pasted on the big screen before them, but he couldn't repeat what was happening on that screen for the life of him. This wasn't the first time the family had gathered in the cabin's theater for a movie night.

He'd enjoyed the other features just fine. But tonight—though the title was one he'd wanted to see—Sawyer was too distracted to focus.

Lounging next to him on the double reclining chair was Betzy. Minutes ago, she'd yawned, stretched, and rolled onto her side to face him. It had been enough to get his pulse to rush. But when she rested her head on his chest, trickled her fingers down his bicep, and looped one of her legs over his, Sawyer could only think of her. Of that kiss they'd shared in the front room. It hadn't been the only kiss they'd shared over the week.

The candy cane kiss, egged on by Duke dangling the mistletoe, was only the beginning. Throughout the days that followed, Betzy's siblings had taken turns showing up with the mistletoe at odd times. They'd even passed the sprig on to Lilly and let her wave it over them as they were lounged before the fire one morning.

Overall, they'd kissed exactly six times since they arrived, but only one of those was shared when the two were alone. Only one had been initiated by them—not Betzy's family. And before they left the cabin, something they planned to do first thing in the morning, Sawyer wanted very badly to repeat that moment.

He needed to know what fueled her on that morning. Needed to know if she'd give in to another moment of passion, when the two of them were alone.

He waited for the movie to end, tuning in to the soft rhythm of her sweet breath. At last the credits rolled. Matthew carried a sleeping Lilly out of the theater while Link held onto his mom's hand, galloping all the way to the exit, which was right beside his and Betzy's seat.

"Tell them goodnight," his mom Emmy said.

"Have a good sleep, Sawyer and Betzy," the kid said.

"You too," he said in return.

"She's out, huh?" Claudia said as she came up behind the small group.

"Yeah," Sawyer answered. "I'll wait until everyone clears out, then I'll get her back to her room."

"I'm sure you will," Duke mumbled as he headed toward the exit as well.

Zander gave the back of Duke's head a slap from behind.

"Goodnight, all," Camila said while snuggling into James.

"I'll wait until you all clear out of here to turn the lights out," came Lorraine.

He'd been wondering where she'd gone off to. Sawyer peered against the gray glow of the screen to see the woman standing beside a switch.

"Go ahead and shut it off," he said. "I think we'll stay here a bit longer before heading back."

"Alright then," she said. "Suit yourself." The room went black save the light pouring in from the hallway. Zander held the door open, allowing everyone to filter out one by one.

Once Lorraine took her exit, Zander peeked his head into the theater. "Night, man. Night, Betz."

"Night," Sawyer said. And then the room went black.

Betzy hadn't said goodnight to Zander in return, but Sawyer was almost positive that the rhythm of her breath had changed. Was she awake at last?

Maybe this was his chance to tell her how he really felt.

The mere thought caused a flare of firecracker heat to pop and jump in his chest. He exhaled a jagged breath, ran a hand up the length of her back, and pressed a kiss to the top of her head.

Of all the kisses he'd kept track of over the days gone by, he hadn't counted those. It simply felt too natural to kiss her forehead after he'd straightened her beanie cap out in the snow. Or to press a kiss to her silky cheek while she strung dried apple rings for the tree's garland. He'd spent the last week of his life loving Betzy the way he wanted to.

Of course, if he knew she could be his—really his—there'd be no stopping him during the late nights that had him aching to step over to the bedroom beside his, tap on her door, and see if she wanted to join him for another fireplace rendezvous.

"Betzy," he whispered under his breath. "I want you in my life, for real."

Her breath stayed steady and paced. He considered saying the next words that poured into his mind. *This has been the best week of my life. When I propose to you, I want it to be for keeps. I want nothing more than to spend the rest of my life with you by my side.*

His pulse shot into super speed at the very thought. Speaking those words out loud was a risk. One that had magnified with each passing year. If Betzy knew how deep his feelings went, and she didn't feel the same, she might panic and call the whole thing off. And then what would his chances be?

And just why in heavens name did he have to turn into that traumatized twelve-year-old boy each time he considered telling her how he felt?

But the answer was clear—Sawyer had let that rejection drive him for more than half of his life. Where Betzy was concerned, he'd done everything he could to become a man she couldn't walk away from. But there was no guarantee.

In fact, what he'd really done, by living the last ten years of his life hoping to impress Betzy and her family, was create a dangerous scenario, one that would leave him hopeless if she didn't feel the same.

Without the hope of having her in his life, Sawyer feared he'd be aimless and alone the rest of his days. The chronic bachelor, like his Uncle Ryan.

Perhaps the next article *Slipper* planned to release, the one about those destined to be rich and all alone, should have been about him.

His pulse pounded harder at the thought.

Just as the inner turmoil threatened to set his body ablaze, Betzy stirred slightly, lifting her head off his chest. "Is the movie over?" she asked.

"Yes." A hot ache rippled through him anew as he considered saying goodbye to moments like these. Her closeness, her touch, her kiss.

If they were to soon be gone, Sawyer may as well make each moment count. Show Betzy how he felt in the quiet night. Assure her that he wasn't faking his feelings for her at all. They were more real than anything he'd known.

With that thought, Sawyer moved a hand to her hip, hoping to get her on the same page.

Betzy made a circle along his chest with the tip of one finger. It triggered that warmth low in his belly once more. That longing to have her lips on his.

"Is everyone else gone?" she asked, trailing another circle over his shirt.

He blew out a jagged breath. "Yes."

Betzy could hardly believe she'd fallen asleep in Sawyer's arms. The truth was, being held in his strong, powerful embrace was a thing of peace. She couldn't imagine a place she'd rather be.

But now that she was awake, and they had the theater to themselves, Betzy planned to take advantage of that fact.

After all, it was their last night at the cabin. Tomorrow, they'd pack up and leave. He'd no longer be one bedroom away from hers. He wouldn't be there to encourage her on the slopes.

To kiss her when mistletoe magically appeared, or to generously hand over the keys to his Lamborghini.

But he was there with her right then, and heaven help her, those warm, strong hands of his were gripping her hips, causing all sorts of chaos and bliss at once.

There was no questioning what was on Sawyer's mind. The chemistry was there—strong and alluring—but was it connected to true and deep feelings, like hers? Or driven by thoughts of simply having a good time, like Duke suggested?

Either way, Betzy couldn't let the moment pass.

Flattening one hand on his chest, she moved in, lowering herself until her mouth was a breath space from his.

Please say he feels the same.

Sawyer's lips parted, ever so slightly, and she dared herself to graze over them in a slow, gentle tease. A wave of bliss rushed through her as she did, back and forth, every tiny touch heightening the anticipation.

At last Betzy pressed her mouth against his, one long, lingering kiss. And then another. There was a certain thrill in being the one to initiate that kiss, found in the blessed return of that affection.

Sawyer's lips were strong and certain, and as they kissed yet again, he surprised her by rolling onto his side until he hovered over her. Shouldering his weight then, he teased the spot just below her earlobe, like he'd done by the fire.

Yes. A new dose of euphoria rushed through her in a heavenly wave.

Sure, Betzy *did* like taking control of the moment. Liked knowing that she could. But as Sawyer took over, rendering her breathless with the slow tease along her throat, she reveled in the knowledge that it was all him.

He was the one initiating every tantalizing kiss.

Each whispered breath.

And every thrilling touch.

At last he made his way to her lips once more. There, Sawyer kissed her in slow succession, reviving waves of bliss with each heavenly push and pull.

Softly then, he brought a hand up to her cheek, cradling her face with a touch so tender, Betzy felt she might cry.

This was love. It had to be. She could feel it swelling deep in her chest. He was telling her, with his actions alone, that he loved her. And she loved him too, wanted to make sure he felt it as well.

Yet just in that moment, a recollection of that text exchange came to mind.

2 grand says you don't even get past second base...

...one step at a time, my friend...

...more of a prude than I thought...

The warmth surrounding her heart went cold in one, frantic beat. What was she thinking? *Fake fiancé with benefits, remember?*

She couldn't assume Sawyer loved her because of a moment like this. Intimacy could be a misleading thing. It meant different things for different people. And somehow Betzy knew that if she let things go too far, recovering from the damage would be more than she could bear.

Sure, Betzy wanted to believe he was kissing her because he felt exactly the same way, but she knew better than that, didn't she? Sawyer, like most of the guys she'd dated, didn't want someone with more money or power than he had. It was what the article was all about. And it was probably right.

With a nagging regret in the back of her mind, Betzy pulled away, putting an end to their kiss. The greater part of her was in flight mode. Something had rocked her mental boat, and she needed to sort through her thoughts before she did something stupid.

"It's late," she breathed against his mouth. She lifted her head to kiss him once more, reminding herself that it might be their last.

Sawyer drew out the kiss with the gentle pull of her bottom lip, then sighed. "Betzy…"

She waited there, feeling vulnerable in the intimate moment, dreading what he might say. Would he ask her to spend the night with him? He might decide it was only fair after all he was doing for her.

He might also be determined to clear things up. *This is just for fun, you know that right? I don't see this going anywhere after we're through.*

Those were words she couldn't fathom hearing. "Let's say goodnight," she blurted before he said anything more.

"I've got something I want—"

"Please, Sawyer. I think it's best if you don't…if we just stay focused on what we're doing here. Okay?"

Sawyer went lax, his form growing heavy for a beat. "Fine. If that's what you'd like," he said, voice raspy and raw.

He sat up slowly, then took her hand to help her do the same. After Betzy climbed down from the chair, she spotted the crack of light beneath the door and walked to it. She swung it wide open, then realized Sawyer was still sitting on the recliner.

"You coming?" she asked, hopeful that he'd still walk her to her room. Still want to hold her hand or rub her back or possibly even kiss her goodnight.

"No," he said. "You go ahead."

Disappointment struck her like sharp darts.

He was angry that she'd stopped things from going further.

What difference did it make? Sawyer was doing what she'd asked him to do. Come next week, he'd propose to her on live TV for the whole country to see. That's what this was for, after all.

But once their time came and went, Betzy would be left with a heart that belonged more to Sawyer than it did her. Over the week, he'd managed to fill nearly every part. Once he left, and she'd trimmed all of those parts away, Betzy had to wonder if there'd be anything left.

CHAPTER 17

Sawyer balled up his fist and gave the leather chair a good hard punch. He'd been so close to saying it, to telling her he loved her, and she'd stopped him.

He shook his head in frustration. She *had* heard him say it the first time, hadn't she? Betzy had heard it, but she'd pretended she hadn't. The reason for that was clear—she didn't feel the same.

His gut twisted anew. Why had he tried to say it again? After she'd dodged it the first time, Sawyer's second attempt had nearly forced her into saying what she didn't want to say. *Sorry, Sawyer. You've done good for yourself, you really have, but I could never be married to someone like you.*

Sawyer was starting to think the article was on to something. If a man like him wasn't good enough for Betzy, if she felt she was somehow still "too rich" for blood like his, perhaps she really was destined to be alone.

He made it back to his room with slow steps. Years of effort, longing, and hope. All of it lay in ruins on that theater chair in the Benton's cabin just days before Christmas.

When he made it to his room at last, Sawyer couldn't fathom the thought of spending another night in that space. Not after it had all been crushed so thoroughly. So he pulled out his phone, arranged for a driver to pick him up, and scribbled out a note to leave on his bed.

Had an emergency to attend to. Just work, not the dog this time. No worries, I'll be there for the live show.

Sawyer stared at the pen as it hovered over the page. If her grandmother saw the note, she'd expect to see the proper farewell, especially since he was supposed to propose to her in just two short days.

A sad sort of grin crossed his lips as he realized that, this time, Betzy couldn't silence him. He'd say it after all.

With that, Sawyer met the paper with his pen once more.

I love you, Betzy Boo.

Sawyer.

He set the page on top of the bed, hiked his bag over one shoulder, and headed out to the family room. It was then he noticed that the fireplace was on.

A foolish spot of hope rose in him as he wondered if Betzy would be sitting in front of it. She wasn't, but her Grandma Lo was.

"Sawyer?" She sat in the firelight's glow on the corner of the couch, arms folded, one leg crossed over the next where it bounced with the tick of the clock. "Leaving so soon?"

He peered into the darkness out the window, knowing his ride wouldn't be there for twenty minutes at least.

"I have to," he said. "But I'll…"

"Keep up your end of the deal?"

Sawyer's stomach dropped. The scarce light showed her position well enough, but it did a poor job of illuminating her face.

"What deal might that be?" he asked.

"She asked you to propose to her. She wants to stuff it in Daisy's face."

Sawyer didn't reply.

"I can't blame her," she said. "I'd have done the same thing. How long are you supposed to stay *engaged?*" She lifted her hands to put finger quotes around the word.

Still, he couldn't get himself to answer. At this point, she didn't seem to have confirmation. Sawyer didn't want to be responsible for giving that to her. He resigned himself to taking a seat on the opposite couch; from there, he shot another longing look out the window.

"I don't think you should do it."

"I can't not—" But then he caught himself. *Crud!* Sawyer clenched his jaw shut tight enough for his teeth to grind.

"This isn't the way to handle the situation. It's not...it's not the Benton way. Jonathon would never approve of it. I'm sure Claudia thinks it's swell. The kids too. But petty tactics like these...you know what they say about playing in the mud."

Sawyer ran a hand along the back of his neck, still cursing himself for blabbing.

"I know it sounds old fashioned, but there's no policy or plan better than honesty. And the honest truth is, Daisy was wrong to put the article out there. I'd rather stand in the right than join her in doing something wrong."

With elbows propped on his knees, Sawyer dropped his face

in his hands. "I know what you mean," he said. "And I know Betzy admires you more than anyone. But if you want to stop all of this, you're barking up the wrong tree."

"No, I'm not," she said. *"You're* the one she's asked to propose to her. On the live taping, is my bet."

Sawyer pulled his hands from his face, his eyes adjusting to the darkness now, and shook his head. "You don't get it. If she wants me to do it, no matter what *it* is, I'll do it. I'd never tell her no." His lower lip threatened to tremble, but he caught hold of the emotion and bit it back. *Just get to the car, man. If you're going to break down, hold out until then.*

"You really do love her, don't you?"

Sawyer turned his gaze on her once more. "More than anything."

"Does Betzy know that?"

He nodded as a humorless laugh bubbled up his throat. "Yep. She sure as...heck does." He might have bit back the curse word at his lips, but there were all sorts of language bombs going off in his head. What a joke the night had been.

"She knows," he assured her. "But she doesn't want to *admit* she knows. Because then she'd have to tell me that, sadly, I'm still not enough for her after all these years." That breakdown threatened to surface once more.

"That hardly sounds like Betzy to me," the woman said.

"Yep. Wish I was wrong about it, but I'm not." A wave of light moved over the room, and Sawyer hopped up and hurried over to the window. Miracle of all miracles, his ride was already there.

"Well," he said in a whisper. "It's been a pleasure. You have a wonderful family. As for the...arrangement, unless you can get

Betzy to change her mind, it's on, and there won't be any stopping it."

She nodded, but stayed in place. "If that's how you feel about it."

He hurried over to the door, pried it open, and twisted the lock behind him. "It is."

CHAPTER 18

Revenge was the name of the game and Betzy wasn't about to lose sight of that again. So what if she wasn't *really* going to marry Sawyer Kingsley? All of America would believe that she was. More importantly, Daisy Shay would believe it, and that *would not* be a hollow reward. Betzy would find total satisfaction as the owners and operators of *Slipper Magazine* bit into that giant piece of humble pie.

This was the only real way to take fate into her own hands. This, unlike Sawyer's feelings for her, was something she could control.

"How does that look?" the makeup artist asked, pulling Betzy back to the present.

Betzy looked into the mirror and primped her hair a bit. Was this the right look? It was hard to say what makeup, hair, and clothes were right for the moment your best friend would become your fake fiancé. On live TV, no less.

Today's episode would feature diverse nonprofit organizations rather than multi-million dollar companies in jeopardy. Organizations that saved lives, focused on the forgotten, and bettered communities across the country. What the guests *didn't* know, was that—on today's show—every contestant would be a winner.

There couldn't be a better platform. Here she was, a billionaire bachelorette, helping one awesome organization after the next, then getting engaged to one of New York's hottest bachelors. One Daisy Shay happened to want for herself.

Betzy knew the thoughts were shallow, knew they didn't really represent her or the life she'd strived to live, but look where those ideals had gotten her. It was time to play the game like everyone else.

"Ms. Benton? Is it good? Would you like anything added or changed?"

Betzy shook her head. "No, sorry. You did a great job. Thank you."

Their last live performance of the show hadn't gone so well. James, bless him, had been struggling with Winston's death the entire year leading up to the episode, which had led him to grab one of the guests by the shirt and scare the living daylights out of him. That wouldn't happen today.

The show's theme song had been replaced with Christmas music. She watched from the curtain's edge, Zander at her side, and smiled at the shift in the overall mood of the crowd.

Good, this was good. It was just what she and Grandma had been aiming for when they planned the special edition. Give the audience members and people at home a feel of Christmas.

Her thoughts veered next to a few of the charities they'd be helping today. While researching the many organizations that applied, Betzy had been moved to tears by the compassion shown. People—normal, everyday people—had put their lives on hold and focused on making the world a better place. Many sacrificed greatly to do so.

Shelters for the homeless were high among them, but there were also groups that focused on Christmas gifts for kids in foster facilities, companionship for the elderly, scholarship programs for the youth.

Just recalling those causes gave Betzy pause for what she was about to do—steal the thunder of the evening with a complete sham.

Stop, Betzy. You have the right to save face. After all, she'd worked as hard as any man in the industry to accomplish what she had over the years. *Harder,* since she was a woman. And look how it had come back to bite her.

Not if she could avoid it.

Milo Jazz, the show's host, welcomed the crowd, his tone different from the exuberant one he usually started out with. James and Duke were, of course, waiting on the other side of the stage for the introductions to begin.

While The Lion's Den had held primetime, seasonal slots for years now, very few of those episodes were filmed live. Thank heavens for that.

"Today we have a very special live edition of The Lion's Den. One that will warm your heart just in time for Christmas. Let's start with the king of the den, always up for an adventure, Mr. Duke Benton."

Duke headed onto the stage with a grin, his man bun perfectly in place.

"You're going to do great, sis," Zander said from behind.

Betzy tossed him a grin over her shoulder. Inwardly, she was nothing but nerves.

"Thanks." She glanced at the teleprompter as Milo continued. And what was this? It looked like there had been a change in Betzy's intro.

"And now for the sensible, the rational, the ultimate taker of the highroad, our lovable Betzy Benton."

The intro change had Grandma's name all over it. *Nice one.* It'd become increasingly clear that the insightful woman was on to her, though she hadn't come out and said so.

Betzy's face flushed hot as she walked onto the stage, tucked her hair behind one ear, and gave her signature wink to the camera. Only this time, she should have directed it to the crowd.

That wink, though Sawyer didn't know it, was for him each and every time. He *had* been the one to teach her to wink. He'd included the fact in his practice proposal to her, and Betzy would give anything to hear him say it all over again. Even if it was just for pretend. The truth was, the events he referred to *were* real, and it seemed that Sawyer treasured the memories as well.

She hadn't been able to see his seat from her spot behind the curtain, but now she could. He was sandwiched between Mom and his own mother, Kellianne, at the upper left corner of the audience. Grandma Lo was there too, seated beside Mom.

Another flash of heat rushed up the front of her neck and pooled into her face. What was she doing? Was she crazy to really go through with such a plan? To expect Sawyer to actually propose to her on live TV a month after he'd been named most eligible bachelor, no less. People might know it was a ploy.

James came out on cue, nodding at the crowd as he did. Boy, did he look happy. And he was. Betzy had noticed a big shift in him since he met Camila, and she was thrilled for him. Thrilled that he'd found the beginning to his happily ever after with such a great woman.

But would her happy ending ever come? And if that ending couldn't be with Sawyer, would she even want it with someone else?

"And now for the lion with the loudest roar, the one who puts *rude* in *shrewd*, it's Zander Benton."

Zander strode out, that famous smolder in check. In business, he was *not* one to reckon with, the audience knew that much. What they didn't know was that, in his personal life, you'd rarely find a kinder human.

The first contestants, a middle-aged couple, stepped onto the stage and explained the charity they'd organized over twelve years ago after losing a child to cancer. Unbeknownst to them, Zander had already selected them out of the bunch as one of his picks.

He played his part by announcing the funds he planned to contribute. He then went on to explain the life-changing arrangements he'd made with the help of other generous supporters in the area—a key element Grandma and all her wisdom insisted on. *It doesn't matter if our means are large or small, everyone should have the gift of making a difference.*

Milo turned the time over to sponsors. When the show picked up once more, the crowd-charming host would bring out James' organization. Then Duke's. And then Betzy's would be up next.

Followed by the proposal. She'd kept her eyes decidedly *off* the upper corner where Sawyer sat, but as their time approached, Betzy allowed her gaze to drift up to that magnetic spot in the crowd.

Sawyer straightened in his seat, meeting her gaze in a blink, and gave her one distinct nod, determination in the tight set of his jaw. *It's on.*

Another burst of heat shoved through her chest. Life for both of them was about to change.

CHAPTER 19

"Can I see the ring?"

The question, poised by Betzy's mother Claudia, took Sawyer off guard. In minutes, once the production came back from commercial, he was supposed to head down the steps and onto the stage, get on one knee, and propose marriage to Betzy on live TV.

Most of the audience members were up on their feet, following Milo's dancing instruction while music boomed—a way of keeping everyone entertained during the break.

Still, Sawyer was careful as he cupped the ring box in one hand. He kept it low on the seat, then pried it open to give Claudia a peek.

Her brow lifted. A smile spread across her lips. And satisfaction rushed through Sawyer in a fast flash.

"That's perfect," she said. "Did she pick it out, or did you?" ·

"Betzy told me the cut she preferred. I took it from there."

The woman nodded. "It's going well so far. The top three tabloids talked about your appearance at the auction. One scored a picture of you two at the vet, and another reported that you'd spent the week with her at the cabin. The groundwork has been laid."

"Right," Sawyer agreed.

"What about the proposal? Do you know what you're going to say?"

"Yep."

"Please tell me Betzy gave you the one she wrote up. You need to say it just as she wrote it."

Sawyer clenched his jaw shut for a blink. "She told me not to."

"Well, you can't wing it on live TV."

"I'm not," he assured.

"Two more dance moves, then we'll go live once again, friends," Milo cheered.

"Whatever you do," Claudia said in a whisper, "just don't draw attention to your childhood together. People will think you're doing her a favor out of loyalty. We need them to think you've fallen in love with the real Betzy. The one they're attacking in that article."

Irritation burned hot within him. He *was* in love with that Betzy. And Sawyer didn't appreciate the last-minute bomb.

Had Betzy put her up to this? They wanted a poised and proper proposal, did they? The kind they might get out of someone who'd been raised in money. Taught to keep up the good family name.

Milo had the crowd take their seats as the countdown

played over the big screen. The noise died down, the cameras zoomed in, and the host welcomed the viewers back at home.

Adrenaline coursed through Sawyer hard enough to catapult him onto the stage in one cannon-like blast. From the corner of his eye, he caught sight of his own leg bouncing. He stopped it quick and forced his next breath to slow through pursed lips.

His mom, who sat on the opposite side of him, rested a hand over his and gave it a reassuring squeeze. He glanced over in time to catch her encouraging smile, one that hadn't quite broken through the tightening in her face.

She was nervous too. Was she worried that he'd do something to upset her friendship with Claudia? Or that he was headed toward the inevitable heartbreak she'd warned him about?

And then there was Claudia's recent direction: avoid bringing up their history. Which was ridiculous since that's where it all began. What her mother really wanted to avoid was *his* past. *His* roots. Where *he* came from.

Fine. The woman wanted Betzy to have a proposal from the man in the magazine, New York's most eligible bachelor? He could give them that easily enough.

Betzy's charity was next on the stage. The restless leg-bouncing came back, but Sawyer could hardly control it. The adrenaline coursing through him demanded an escape. He could feel the heat of Grandma Lo's gaze, a plea for him to put all this to a halt. Sadly, he couldn't comply.

The audience began to cheer suddenly, alerting Sawyer to the happenings on stage. Betzy stood up to accept an embrace from the guest she planned to sponsor.

Sawyer put his hands together as well, offering a preemptive prayer to the heavens. *Forgive me. But I love her.*

And suddenly he was up on his feet.

Taking the shallow steps toward the front of the stage.

He locked eyes with Milo through the chaos and crowd. *It's time.*

"And what is this?" the host said after ushering their latest guest backstage. He patted his sweater vest theatrically before looking over the crowd in feigned confusion. "Did I lose a cue card? Are we doing something…" At this point, just as planned, a guy from the stage crew brought Sawyer a mic.

Sawyer tested it with a tap, then brought it to his lips. "You didn't miss a cue card," he assured. "But if you don't mind, I've got something I'd like to do."

Betzy had taken a seat in her chair once more. Sawyer approached it with short steps as a hush fell over the crowd. His pulse echoed in his ears as he stood before her.

Slowly then, Sawyer lowered himself to one knee.

Whispered chatter, mixed with oohs and ahs, buzzed throughout the crowd.

A Benton-worthy man, he reminded himself as Claudia's words shot back to his mind. Sawyer gulped through the tightness in his chest, then reached out and took hold of her hand.

"Betzy," he started. From across the studio, she'd appeared calm and poised, but as he sandwiched her small hand in his, Sawyer saw that she was trembling.

She met his gaze, her eyes brimming with a reservation that gave him pause. He kept his focus fixed on her face, watching as her lips parted the slightest bit.

His heart clanked hard out of beat. Was she about to stop things? Somehow signal him to call the whole thing off?

Only she didn't. She simply glanced over the crowd, moistened her lips, and set those piercing blue eyes back on him. He squeezed her hand, and reveled in the appearance of those dimples in her cheeks.

That smile.

The energy darting through him shifted at once. Betzy's hand stopped trembling in his grip. *This* was what they needed. A reminder of what the two shared, a connection that existed, audience or no.

He'd conjured a bland proposal that might have satisfied her mom, the audience members, and naysayers alike. But those weren't the words he wanted to speak.

Sawyer had worked most of his life to be worthy of this moment, and he wasn't about to hide where he came from. Where he had been. And the fact that he'd loved this girl from clear back when.

"When I was eight years old, I fell for the cutest girl. She liked math, which I thought was weird. She liked fast cars, which I thought was awesome. And she also liked me, which I thought made perfect sense."

Betzy giggled, dabbing a fingertip to the corner of her eye as moisture built there.

"And now, twenty years later, I'm in love with that same girl, only she's kind of different too. She has a head for business, which is as cool as it is intimidating. She has a heart for others, so big she can't hide it even when she tries. And somehow..." He shook his head, daring himself to speak what he wanted to say. "Somehow she likes me too—the son of her

164

childhood housemaid—which I realize now doesn't make any sense."

Murmurs broke out over the crowd.

"But that's what makes it right," he explained. "That's what makes what we have...*real*. It never made sense for us to be together, but I miss you every day that we're apart."

He tugged the ring box from his pocket and flicked it open. Cameras he'd forgotten were there came close to zoom in on the diamond, one fit for a queen.

"I don't want us to live apart anymore. I want to start a life together. The one we always dreamed of. So, Betzy Benton, will you do me the honor of becoming my bride?"

A blanket of pin-drop silence fell over the crowd.

He felt exposed once the words were all out. Naked in front of the world. Sure, the proposal was part of the plan, but he'd never expected it to feel so real.

Betzy dabbed the corners of her eyes, shifted and stood to her feet, then nodded before the word escaped her lips. "Yes," she finally said.

The crowd's reaction rivaled that of a NASCAR win by Mario Andretti himself. Sawyer straightened to his feet, pulled Betzy into his arms, and reveled in the warmth and comfort of her there. He brought his lips to her ear, whispered through the noise of the crowd.

"I love you."

Betzy's grasp loosened enough for her to lean back and face him. She studied him for a blink. Her eyes flickered to the nearby cameras, and then back to him.

"I love you, too."

A chaotic thrill pushed through his insides, louder than the applause. *It's all for the cameras,* he reminded himself. The audience cheered some more as he slipped the ring onto her finger.

Sawyer leaned in to seal it with a kiss. Short, and painfully sweet. It was likely the last time their lips would touch.

Music picked up, and suddenly Milo was closing the segment, asking viewers to support their local charities, and wishing all a merry Christmas.

The proposal had gone off perfect, at least from Sawyer's perspective, but Milo's words brought with him a sober realization. It was almost Christmas. Soon Sawyer would board a flight and go back to the life he'd planned on leaving behind.

As Sawyer joined the Bentons in waving to the audience, Betzy looped her arm through his and cuddled up to him. And though he tried to avoid it, his gaze drifted up to the corner where some very important women stood.

Mom's face was covered with tears, but they didn't mask the concern. Claudia on the other hand, was a woman trained in the art of composure. Chin lifted, eyes barely glistening with tears, and a pleased smile on her face. If Betzy's mom was ticked off at him, and she definitely was, she knew how to mask it.

And then came a woman who was equally angry with him. The one Sawyer did not want to meet eyes with, yet he did it all the same. Lorraine Benton looked nearly as poised as Claudia. Yet as she clapped, waved back to the stage, and kept a grip on that unwavering grin, he caught the barely perceptible shake of her head.

A hot streak of fear shot through him as he realized just how real this was. He'd just proposed to Betzy on live TV, there was no taking it back. Sadly, the engagement itself was fake all the same.

Talk about an emotional storm. Hope clashing with doubt. Disappointment replacing moments of bliss. Love persisting through the deepest ache.

And now, as the countdown ended in the live production, one prominent question cried out in Sawyer's mind.

What did I get myself into?

CHAPTER 20

*B*etzy pressed her hands to her temples. If she clenched her eyes tight enough, maybe the horrible sight before her would disappear.

She'd made a mistake. Oh, had she ever made a mistake. Betzy had undermined Daisy Shay and what she was capable of, and now she would pay a price—the front-page news had made sure of it.

"I told you this was a bad idea," Grandma said to Mom, confirming that she'd been onto them all along.

"You didn't have anything better," Mom snapped.

A hand rubbed along Betzy's shoulder a moment before Camila spoke up. "Do you want anything? Coffee? A box of tissues?"

"A sledgehammer," Rachel suggested.

Sledgehammer? "For what?" Betzy pulled her hands from her face to peer up at her friend who, like the rest of the women, was gathered around her kitchen table for an emergency meeting. One that started at 5:30 in the morning after Grandma Lo stumbled onto her porch to collect her newspaper.

Rachel shrugged. "To get out your aggression?"

"I forgot that the Shays have family in the newspaper business too," Mom grumbled.

"Maybe you shouldn't torture yourself with this anymore," Camila suggested. Her sister-in-law proceeded to pin the corner of the newspaper between her finger and thumb, but Betzy flattened her hand over it.

"It's six in the morning," Betzy said. "I think I should be able to torture myself until..." She glanced at the clock on the microwave. "Noon."

She hovered over the paper once more. There, screaming from the front page, were three damning words in bold print: *It's a Sham!*

Below, pictures of their engagement showed just what *it* referred to. She glanced over the images with a heavy sigh. Sawyer was on one knee in the first picture.

Her heart ached anew.

Next was a picture of the two embracing after he'd asked her to marry him.

What a moment that had been.

The third showed Sawyer sliding the engagement ring onto her finger, a ring that Betzy hadn't wanted to remove until she caught sight of the very last picture on that page.

Before setting her eyes on the dreaded sight, Betzy reread the explanation of the photo, printed just alongside.

Cheating bachelor with old high school flame, Daisy Shay, just days before engagement.

And there it was for all eyes to see. Daisy and Sawyer kissing in some stupid bar.

If Betzy hadn't seen it with her own eyes, she wouldn't have believed it. She'd tried writing it off with the timing alone. Heck, he'd been with her at the cabin for the entire week. But he'd left before everyone else, on a dark night, all by himself. And it just so happened that he'd left in an angry huff after Betzy slowed things down between them. Looks like he knew where to get what he wanted after all.

"Good riddance," she spat while glaring at the page. "They deserve each other." Acid swooshed through her body in a boiling rage. But it wasn't anger that prevailed. The hurt—that was heavier, hotter, greater.

Hurt from having lost Sawyer, officially, once and for all. Not that she'd ever really had him, she realized.

And that's when the shame settled in. Reminding Betzy that she'd done this to herself. A jagged whimper cracked in her throat as she covered the sight with her hands. She wanted nothing more than to climb back into bed and never come out. "I've never felt so miserable in my life."

"Five copies of *Slipper Magazine* at your service," Matthew said as he came in from the back door. He handed the stack to Claudia before shrugging out of his coat.

"How bad is it?" Claudia asked while thumbing past the first few pages.

Grandma took one and passed on the rest. "Yeah, did you read it yet?"

Matthew shook his head. "No, I was driving. I'll leave that to *you* guys."

Camila took one and handed the other two to Betzy. Rachel

snatched her copy, gave her finger a lick, and began flicking the pages.

Betzy stared at the cover, not quite willing to dive into her magazine just yet. "First one to find it, call out the page, will you?"

"Twenty-three," Camila said. Betzy looked down to Camila's magazine to see the exact spread she'd been sent anonymously.

"This is what I saw," Betzy explained.

Yep. It was all there. Just as evil as she remembered. *Worse*, she realized as she read over the longer pieces of text. Not all were quotes from her ex-boyfriend. Some were mere observations about her behavior. Each trait, when combined with the others, created a long list that matched up with dozens of wealthy spinsters who never married.

The article tore open her greatest fear with razor sharp, fire hot veracity. She really would be alone forever, wouldn't she?

"I can see why you did what you did," Grandma said. "This is infuriating! And just how in the world did they get hold of that marriage contract? That's clear back from the time you were kids."

"Huh?" Betzy reached over and flicked the page. And there it was. The exact document they'd typed up twenty years ago. Sawyer's messy signature with the wavy 'y'. And hers on the line beneath it.

She groaned. "We said we'd get married when we were twenty-eight. Guess how old I am right now?"

"You're twenty-eight," Matthew said while fiddling with the coffee pot.

"Could I have made myself look *more* pathetic? They're making it look like I was actually holding him to it."

"Aw, honey," Grandma started to say, but even she knew this was beyond fixing.

The lights were flickering. At least from her perspective. And the air around her was getting thick and hazy. Betzy put a hand up.

"I just need to get back in my bed for a minute." If a minute meant the rest of her life.

"I'm not sure that's the best idea, Betz," Mom said.

"It *is*," she assured while climbing off the chair. She shuffled her aching body away from the table, trying to see past the hectic haze in her head. "Just...give me some time please. Help yourself to coffee."

As she made her way to the bedroom, Betzy overheard Mom announce that Daisy would be appearing on one of the morning shows. *Great.*

Score one for Grandma, who'd somehow known Betzy's plan was the worst idea ever. Score another one for Grandma, since she'd warned Betzy that Sawyer might actually be among the dirt bags of the universe, something Betzy still couldn't fathom despite the evidence she'd seen in black and white.

She climbed back into bed in her still-dark room, pulled the covers high over her head, and let the pain have its way with her.

It felt like someone was shredding her heart with a cheese grater. Piece by tiny piece.

If Sawyer planned to go off and conspire with the enemy, why hadn't he just waited a few months? Why commit to doing something and then mess it all up? Why act like he wanted to defend her when what he did instead was make everything a million times worse?

On top of it all, Sawyer had broken her heart. Ruined her trust. And destroyed her hope for a happy ending.

If Sawyer Kingsley wasn't the man she thought he'd been all along, the man who allowed her to still have faith in men outside of her own family, what did she have left to hope for?

"Are you sure this is a good idea?" Camila asked through the phone line.

"I think it's the *best* idea," Betzy answered as she made her way up the ramp and onto the jet, phone propped to her ear. "It's what James did, and look how well that turned out."

"True," Camila said through the line. "I just worry that you're going all alone."

Betzy appreciated her sister-in-law's concern. "Maybe I'll request a male personal chef. A single Italian who somehow knows how to massage stress knots out of a broken woman's back." She lifted her sunglasses to rest on her head and took a seat in one of the leather lounge chairs. Her eyes moved to the wet bar where her favorite seltzer water chilled.

"You're not broken," Camila assured. "You've just got a few cracks."

"Whatever I am," Betzy said as a fresh ache tore through her chest, "I want to hurry and move on to the next phase. The healed instead of the healing. The mended instead of the cracked."

A sigh came through the line. "Betzy?"

She pressed the phone more snugly against her ear. "Yeah?"

"We all have cracks," Camila assured. "But we're like clay jars, right?"

"Huh?"

"The clay jars that hold candles. The cracks are good. Without them, no light shines through."

She gave that some thought as Camila continued.

"Your family has endured so much. Yet you still shine light in so many different directions. It's inspiring."

Betzy let herself sit in that for a moment, gleaning slivers of comfort from the words. "Thanks, Camila. You've inspired me too, you really have." It was true. She admired the way Camila, despite having come from small means, had gone after her dream, pursued greatness, and walked among the very best in her industry. Just like Sawyer.

"You still haven't talked to him?" Camila asked.

Betzy shook her head. "No."

It hadn't been easy, but between the security crew at her estate and the new phone line she'd switched to, Betzy had successfully dodged Sawyer for the entire day. Dodged him and his attempts to apologize for ruining her life, which she could only assume he'd do since he hadn't gotten through.

And now here she was, twelve hours after the vicious discovery of her front-page news, boarding a jet to Italy on her own.

"I'm not *going* to talk to him, either," she added. "There's nothing to say. He and Daisy can have each other. I'm going to go silent for a while, something I probably should have done in the first place."

"Well," Camila said with a sniff. "Enjoy Italy, sweet friend. It's already Christmas Eve over there."

Betzy glanced at her clock. Six p.m. here meant two a.m. there. "Yeah," she said. "I guess it is." She fought back a new wave of sadness. Christmas Day would be close behind it, and Betzy had chosen to spend it all alone.

At least she had a family that respected that.

"Thanks for understanding," she said. "You and James have a merry Christmas."

"Thanks, Betzy. Have a safe flight."

As she disconnected the call, an image of that stupid bar kiss —the one between Daisy and Sawyer—burst into her mind. *Why?* Why was she so set on torturing herself?

Only Betzy realized it was probably more of a defense mechanism. An attempt to finally grasp the reality of a situation she'd refused to see all these years; Sawyer didn't love her. He wasn't dying to come home to her. And they never would have that future she hoped they might.

Yet as she assured herself of that very thing, determined to accept it, mourn, and then hopefully heal from it all, a conflicting recollection came to mind. Sawyer's fervent whisper after he'd proposed. Three glorious words, words that neither the cameras nor the audience could have caught.

I love you.

CHAPTER 21

*S*awyer parked alongside the quiet street, accented by green garlands and hanging lights. Most people were tucked into their homes by now, celebrating with family and friends. But Sawyer had work to do. Or, as it was, one last dragon to slay for his queen.

So here he was, hoping to find Betzy and set the record straight. Sawyer's mother had spoken with Claudia, who'd said he might find Lorraine at her wedding boutique. Lorraine may or may not tell him where to find Betzy, but he had to try.

Sawyer's day had been a maddening one to say the least. Waking to the terrible sight of the front-page news. Seeing *Slipper's* article for himself, realizing that the proposal had, in fact, caused more damage than good.

Of all the infuriating things he'd run into that day, the picture with Daisy Shay was the worst. It had taken a whole lot of phone calls, and the pulling of a whole lot of strings to get results so close to Christmas, but at last Sawyer had what he needed to clear up his name.

At some point, he'd do so in public. But what mattered now was finding Betzy.

At first glance, the sight of the boutique, housed in an old restored mansion, was promising. Warm, glowing light poured from every main floor window. As he took the short flight of stairs up to the porch, Sawyer caught a better look inside. Silk dresses that went on for miles.

A mannequin up front displayed one by itself, and Sawyer wasn't sure why, but the sight caused an odd longing to stir within him. As if Betzy herself was wearing the dress.

Hadn't he just poured his heart out in a proposal for the world to see? There'd been a part of him that believed it might really happen. And somewhere, buried beneath a whole lot of disappointment and doubt, that flicker of hope still burned.

Aside from the lights, there were no signs of life inside the boutique. The sign out front read *closed*. There were no employees to be seen. No noise seeping through the windows or doors. But still, Sawyer lifted his hand and knocked. *Please, Lord, help me find her tonight.*

He tucked his hands into his pockets and shivered. There wasn't snow in this part of the sunshine state, but it wasn't a warm night by any means.

When no one came to the door, hints of despair crept in. Sawyer couldn't let another whole day go by—especially when that day was Christmas Eve—with Betzy believing such horrible things about him.

He pulled a hand from his pocket and knocked one more time.

Longingly, he stared at the handle, willing it to move. Another minute ticked on.

Nothing.

Perhaps he'd try her house once more.

Sawyer spun on one foot, took a step away from the door, and heard a small creak from inside the structure. His pulse spiked as he spun around in time to see that handle twist after all.

He thanked the heavens above as a wedge of light appeared in the open gap. And there, silhouetted against the brightness, was Lorraine.

"Sawyer," she said. "I thought you might come." She stepped aside and motioned for him to come in.

"Thank you," he said, giving the shop a once over. "This is a beautiful place you have here."

She grinned. "Thank you. I think so."

He nodded, rubbed a hand along the back of his neck, and looked into the woman's blue eyes. No use beating around the bush. "I need to find Betzy. Can you help me?"

"I might be able to," she said. "It depends. Let me guess—you've got some way to magically make all of this go away?"

Sawyer shook his head. "No, I can't do that." For a moment, he thought he saw disappointment in her eyes, but her expression smoothed once more.

"So?"

"I can't make all of it go away, but I *can* clear up my side of things by proving that I was *not* with Daisy that night. In fact, since I happen to have some connections of my own back in New York, I scored the actual video footage where that shot was taken from."

The expression she pulled was one he'd seen on Betzy several times. The quick lift of one brow. "You do?"

He nodded. "Daisy came onto me at a bar when she flew out for the article. I'm the one who stopped it. Then she accused me of waiting around for Betzy, asking if *she* was the reason I'd remained single. I didn't argue."

More brow lifting. "Huh. You don't say?"

This time Sawyer couldn't read her expression so well. He tried to gulp back the dryness in his throat. "So can you help me find her?"

"*Have* you been waiting for Betzy all these years?" she asked.

There was no point in denying it now. "Yes."

"Hmm." Lorraine nodded, her face thoughtful. "Do you remember the year you flew your mom out for Christmas?"

Sawyer furrowed his brow. "Yes."

"Betzy flew out to New York on New Years. She saw some woman kiss you in a glass elevator."

The new piece of information was an explosion in his mind, sending questions in every direction. "She did? Why?"

"She didn't think you were seeing anyone at the time, since you'd said you'd be spending the night alone."

"Oh man," Sawyer blurted as he recalled that night. It was just before she started dating Marcus. "Yes, that was a woman from my apartment building. Jane. Her name was Jane. A real man chaser. I told her I was going to bring in the New Year alone, and she leaned in, kissed me, and wished me a Happy New Year. That was it."

The woman nodded some more, thoughtful. Sawyer was doing an awful lot of thinking himself. Betzy had come out to New York? That was just after the double funeral, when he had sensed their relationship shifting into something more. Perhaps she really had been on the same page.

But what now?

Lorraine dabbed at the corners of her eyes. "I liked what you said when you proposed to her," she said. "You didn't take my daughter's advice."

"I know. I couldn't."

"I'm glad," she admitted. "Was what you said true?"

"Yes. All of it."

She nodded, sniffed, and snatched a tissue from a nearby box. She dabbed her eyes and nose. "These come in handy here."

He grinned. " I bet they do." Sawyer could only imagine the tears his own mother would shed on his wedding day. And the days leading up to it while seeing him in his tux, or gazing at his bride-to-be in her dress, something she'd probably get to see before he did.

Lorraine walked around the counter and plucked a set of keys off a decorative hook. "Okay," she said. "Let's go."

"Where are we—"

"Oh," she blurted, throwing a finger in the air. "But first. Just out of curiosity…" Lorraine motioned to a line of mannequins displayed throughout the foyer. There were five in total. "Which of these looks like Betzy to you?"

Sawyer's brow furrowed for a beat, but he indulged her just the same, inspecting one wedding gown after the next. By the time he got to the third dress, he realized it was the one he'd spotted through the window. The one that had him seeing Betzy taking that long walk down the aisle as his very own bride.

"That one," he said, pointing it out for her.

He glanced over to see a slow grin pull at one side of her lips. She lifted one hand to her face and sniffed. "Fate takes the wheel once again," she said in a whisper. At once, she snatched an overcoat off the counter. "Let's get going. Do you have a passport?"

"Of course, but where are we going?"

Lorraine shoved an arm into the sleeve of her coat. Sawyer hurried over to help her with the other side.

Once he'd lifted it over her shoulders, she spun back to face him with a wide grin. "We're going to get Betzy."

CHAPTER 22

The family's restored Italian farmhouse wasn't quite as cozy as Betzy remembered. Of course, it was empty. Plus, it'd been years since she'd been here. In fact, they'd only come once since the plane crash. And it'd been a difficult visit.

After all, Grandpa and Dad had put so many of their own touches on the old place. Transformed the structure from forgotten farmhouse to spacious villa, complete with eight bedrooms, four bathrooms, and one glorious kitchen. Not to mention the guest house sitting on the same property.

A lot of house for one lone girl.

One bitter girl who'd done a fine job of ruining her life. It occurred to her during her long flight from LA to Venice that she'd finally gotten an answer to an almost lifelong question: Were she and Sawyer really meant to be together?

Not only had Betzy gotten the exact answer she didn't want

to get, she'd received it in the worst possible way, complete with public humiliation and all. Joshua, her public relations rep, was working overtime trying to come up with a perfect reply to the accusations that she'd bribed the bachelor into proposing to her.

She'd asked Joshua to refrain from commenting at this time. What could she say? In a way, Betzy had done that very thing. Minus the bribe, of course.

"Christmas Eve," she said to the open space. "It's *Christmas Eve*." She was racking up the tally on botched holidays and last-minute flights. First the crappy trip over New Years, and now this.

Betzy hadn't thought it'd be possible to sleep on the flight over, but sleep she had. During most of the trip, in fact, her body too exhausted to endure the turmoil.

Yet as she sat in the bright, open sunroom, eyeing the endless stretch of nearby villas and the ocean view, Betzy started to wish she hadn't slept at all. Because what was she supposed to do now? It was Christmas Eve and she was all alone, thousands of miles from home, and even further from finding the love she longed for.

She grabbed the remote, flicked on the flat screen, and surfed past at least two-dozen triggers before settling on a music station instead. Then, as Christmas tunes lulled her into memories of her past, Betzy watched the room slowly slip through the twilight glow, and eventually, into darkness.

Lights began popping up from the villas stacked along the hillside. One brave soul sailed along the ocean, his boat lit up with Christmas lights as he moved close to the shore.

Suddenly, she heard a distinct creaking sound come from... she couldn't tell where. At once, Betzy stood to her feet, worrying that she wasn't, in fact, alone as she'd thought. Was it possible someone had been tucked into the upper quarters of the home all this time? Perhaps someone had been staying in the nearby guesthouse.

The creaking came again, and then again, sounding at a rhythmic pace.

The chances of anyone getting past the security system were slim, but even still, Betzy climbed off the couch, moved slowly to the fireplace, and reached for one of the fire pokers.

The sharp sound of iron on iron briefly cut through the rhythmic creak, but then it picked back up again.

"Betzy!" called a male voice from beyond the glass.

A flare of fire burst in her chest. *That voice...*

"No way." Betzy crossed the room in a hurry and moved into the dining area, which offered a view of their private yard. Dad had restored the tall, old-fashioned swing set out back in hopes that the grandchildren would soon come.

They hadn't yet, but there was definitely somebody swinging out there just the same. Outdoor lights lit the area, making it clear to see. She squinted to see beyond the distance, positive she must be dreaming.

The uninvited guest called out once more. "Betzy Boo! Come swing with me."

The poker slipped from her hand and hit the rug with a clank. This was impossible. There was no way Sawyer Kingsley was here in Italy with her. Perhaps she'd fallen asleep after all.

"Betzy," he called again.

Excitement bubbled around her heart. In a rush, she hurried over to the door, pulled it open, and darted outside. Once her feet hit the cold ground, Betzy spun back around to grab her shoes.

She shoved one foot into the ankle boot as she walked, then stepped into the other before hurrying toward the back part of the property.

"Sawyer?" she hollered.

"Come swing with me," he prompted again.

She shook her head, staring at the sight before her in shock. "What is this?"

Hadn't she just seen proof that he was pursuing Daisy Shay? Betzy wanted to hold onto her anger and doubt, but she couldn't. Sawyer had flown all the way out to Venice on Christmas Eve to find her. That outrageous detail replaced those threads of doubt with a growing rush of hope.

"This is me trying to remind you of who I am, because it seems like you forgot." At once Sawyer jumped out of the swing and into the night. He landed flat on his feet like a panther, and straightened his tall, impressive form. "I came here to tell you that Daisy lied. A fact that shouldn't be too shocking, if you think about it; she was trying to save face."

The outdoor light poured over his sculpted jaw as he approached. Those hazel eyes captured the glow in tones of gold.

"Will you let me show you?" he asked.

Betzy could only shake her head. The shock hadn't worn off. In fact, it was only now just settling in. "I can't believe you're here," she said.

A soft smile crossed over his handsome face. "So…is that a yes, no, maybe so?"

"Yes," she blurted. "Come inside." Was it possible he could really combat Daisy's accusation? Betzy couldn't imagine how.

It occurred to her, as she led him into the home, that none of the indoor lights were on, save the small, automatic lamp glowing in the corner. She flicked on lights—the fireplace too— and joined him on the couch. And though Sawyer had been outside longer than she had, he felt warm by her side.

"Hi," he rasped as their eyes met.

A thrill rushed through her. "Hi."

Sawyer tugged his phone from his pocket, eyes narrowing as he swiped, then tapped at the screen. "First things first," he said, tilting the phone so they could both view it.

"The bar picture. It was actually taken during Daisy's visit to the city when she came out for my interview and shoot."

Betzy lifted a brow. "She came out there?"

He nodded, then hit play on the video. The angle said it was surveillance footage. There they were, sitting in the very place portrayed in the front-page photo.

Daisy leaned into him and traced a finger under his chin.

Sawyer smiled but backed away. They talked a bit more it seemed, and then suddenly Daisy was leaning in, wrapping her hand around his neck and kissing him.

"Wow, that was quick," she said.

Even quicker was the pace at which Sawyer pulled back, resting his hand on her shoulder in return. He shook his head, scratched a hand along his jaw, and reached for his drink.

The two spoke some more, and then Daisy came to a stand

and snatched her bag off the nearby chair, hollering something to the bartender as he approached.

Betzy could hardly believe her eyes. "I can't believe she used a shot from *that* scene."

"It's all she had," Sawyer said with a shrug. "I'm afraid that moment might have set things in motion," he said. "See, back in high school, I told her about that little contract we wrote up. When she didn't believe me, I texted her proof of it. A detail I forgot until it appeared in the article." He shook his head. "Anyway, because of everything I'd told her in the past, Daisy guessed why I wasn't interested in her. She knew where my heart was."

That last comment felt like a promise. "And where was it?" she asked, hope filling her chest once more.

"With you, of course. It's always been you."

A million parades marched in the beats of her heart, each heated thump filling her with an added burst of joy. "Really?"

Sawyer nodded, slipped a hand up the side of her neck, and kissed her.

Betzy had barely tuned in to the bliss of that kiss when he pulled back the slightest bit to speak against her lips. "I'm sorry I waited so long," he said before kissing her again.

That brought another question to mind. One she asked after relishing his kiss a moment longer.

"Why *did* you take so long?"

He kissed her lips once more before pulling back to meet her gaze. "Long story short, I was an idiot," he said. "I just...kept telling myself that I wasn't enough for someone like you."

"Sawyer," she said, searching his face. "You've *always* been enough. *More* than enough. You're the one I always dreamt of being with."

He grinned. "You have no idea how nice it is to hear that. Especially since we don't have an audience. Oh, except the one hiding outside, but I'm sure they can't hear what we're saying."

Betzy tipped her head. *"What* audience?"

"Your family's here. And mine too."

Her eyes widened at the news. "You're kidding."

Sawyer's phone buzzed. He glanced down to look at it. "No, I'm not kidding. And they're already asking if they can come in. They're probably worried about the two of us giving the kids a show."

A fresh dash of excitement stirred in her heart. "Lilly and Link are here too?"

Sawyer nodded. "They sure are."

A laugh sounded in her throat as Betzy came to a stand. "Oh my goodness, yes. Tell them to come in!" She spun to face the door when Sawyer spoke up from his spot on the couch.

"Maybe we should have taken a few more minutes to ourselves," he said with a laugh. "I was just getting started."

Betzy spun back around and took hold of his hand. "I'll make sure we get some time alone," she promised.

At once, the door swung open. "Ho, ho, ho!" Duke boomed as he stepped inside with fists full of suitcases and bags.

Zander was just behind him, Lilly in one arm, Link's hand in the other.

"Thanks for making me carry your luggage, chump," Duke grumbled.

"Hey," Zander said with a shrug. "If the kids liked you, we could have done this in reverse."

Duke rolled his eyes. "Kids hate me."

"*I* don't hate you," Lilly promised. "I just like Zan Zan better."

A huge grin came over Duke's face. "Zan Zan?"

"Shut up, man," Zander warned, "or I'll tell everyone the news."

"Let me see the happy couple," Kellianne crooned as she came in next. Her boyfriend, Ted, trailed behind, carting luggage of his own.

She hurried over to Betzy and gave her an exuberant hug. "Oh, dear," she mumbled, pulling back to look her in the face. "Is everything all settled then?"

Betzy looked around the room, spotting her mom, Matthew, and Grandma Lo. James and Camila were there too, all of them seeming to wait for the answer to Kellianne's question.

Joy, gratitude, and excitement rushed through her at the glorious sight of them. "Yes," Betzy announced with a grin.

"I'm so glad," Kellianne gushed, pulling her in for another hug. She pulled Sawyer into the embrace and sighed. "I'm so happy for you two."

"So am I!" squealed Lilly.

The rest of the family members greeted them with hugs and words of congratulations. "Does that mean you guys are going to get married for real?" Lilly asked as she skipped circles around them.

"I hope so," Betzy said, turning to look at Sawyer. "I did say *yes.*"

Sawyer held her gaze, seeming to register what she was saying. "Yes, you did. And we've already waited a very long time to get to this point."

She bit at her lip and grinned. "Short engagement?"

Sawyer grinned back. "Christmas wedding? In Italy?"

Betzy scanned the room for Grandma Lo. She spotted her in the corner of the room, a knowing look on her face as she pointed a thumb to her side.

She glanced over to see that Matthew held one of the boutique's gowns, the logo on the zipped bag making it clear. A gasp pulled from her throat as Betzy looked back at her grandma.

"Is it?" she asked, chills rippling up her arms.

"It is," Grandma assured with a smile.

Betzy turned back to Sawyer. "Let's do it."

At once, he pulled her into his arms and lifted her off the ground. "I can't wait."

"A Christmas wedding in Italy it is," Grandma cheered.

Betzy sighed as Sawyer kissed her once again. She assured herself that their time alone was coming at last; she could hardly wait. They did have a guesthouse, after all.

For now, it seemed as if she had a wedding to plan.

"I'll contact the local preacher," she heard her mom say.

"I'll take care of the food," Camila offered.

Betzy gave Sawyer one more kiss before joining the cluster of improvised wedding planners.

Duke pressed his hands to his cheeks. "I'll paint everybody's nails," he joked.

"Do mine first!" Lilly said, hopping up and down.

Matthew pointed a finger at Duke. "She'll hold you to that."

"Great," Duke grumbled with an eye roll. "At least if *I* end up having to get married, I'll know that Betzy's wedding arrangement was crazier than mine."

Betzy moved her gaze from Duke to Zander, recalling the wedding game show he'd mentioned at the cabin. Was that actually a real thing?

"How does it feel?" Grandma asked, coming up beside her.

Betzy tore her thoughts back to the present. "How does *what* feel?"

A knowing grin tugged at one corner of her mouth. "When fate takes hold of the wheel?"

Betzy gave that some thought, realizing that, as much as she liked being in the driver's seat, she didn't always steer things in the right direction.

Yet somehow, despite the ruins she'd raced into, things were turning out just as she'd dreamed.

A deep rush of gratitude pooled into her heart, so full she couldn't contain it. She pictured her father up in the heavens, with Grandpa and Winston at his side. Perhaps they had a bit of pull. It seemed that what Grandma had been trying to tell her was true after all.

With that acknowledgment running through her mind, she wrapped an arm around her grandma, locked her eyes on Sawyer through the small crowd, and gave her an honest answer.

"It feels…better than I ever imagined."

THE END

***

.   .   .

Thank you for reading Her Best Friend Fake Fiancé.

Watch for the Benton Brothers Romance Series to continue. James' book, 28 Days with a Billionaire, can be found on Amazon now. Zander and Duke will get their happy ending soon, so watch for those releases as well.

FREE BOOK

Subscribe to my newsletter and receive my novella, Ranch

Hand for Auction, FREE as a thank you gift! Simple go to https://dl.bookfunnel.com/9yd9cwg0w2

ALSO BY KIMBERLY KREY

Unlikely Cowgirl Series

Her Gun-shy Cowboy

Her Kismet Cowboy

Her Dream Cowboy

Cobble Creek Small Town Romance

The Unlikely Bride

The Hopeful Bride

The Determined Bride

The Sweet Montana Bride Series

Reese's Cowboy Kiss

Jade's Cowboy Crush

Cassie's Cowboy Crave

Second Chances Series

Rough Edges

Mending Hearts

Fresh Starts

Beach Romance

Catching Waves: A Sweet Beach Romance (The Royal Palm Resort Book 2)

28 days with a Billionaire

Young Adult Novellas

Getting Kole for Christmas

Getting Micah under the Mistletoe

Chemistry of a Kiss

Novella

Ranch Hand for Auction

Navy SEALs Romance

The Honorable Warrior

The Fearless Warrior

Christmas Romance

Her TV Bachelor Fake Fiancé

Her Best Friend Fake Fiancé

The Comfy Christmas Collection: Four Holiday Romance Reads; First
Loves & Second Chances

Collections

Falling for Her Bodyguard: Four Full-length Romance Novels

Cobble Creek Romance Collection: Three small-town Romances

The Sweet Montana Bride Series: Three Witness Protection Cowboy
Romances

Second Chance Romance Series: Three Sweet Romances Featuring
Second Chances

The Comfy Christmas Collection: Four Holiday Romance Reads; First

Loves & Second Chances

It All Starts Here: Sweet Romance Collection: 3 Stand-Alone Series Starters

<u>Also See</u>

The Cowboy's Catch (in Big Sky Anthology)

ABOUT THE AUTHOR

Writing Romance That's Clean Without Losing the Steam!

Award-winning author Kimberly Krey specializes in writing 'Romance That's Clean without Losing the Steam'. She's a fervent lover of God, family, and cheese platters, as well as the ultimate hater of laundry. Follow her on any of the sites below for updates on new releases and or giveaways.

facebook.com/kimberlykreyauthor

twitter.com/KimberlyKrey

instagram.com/romance_is_write

bookbub.com/profile/kimberly-krey

Made in the USA
Coppell, TX
31 December 2022

10146842R00121